Boo'd Up with A Goon From Lil Haiti

By: Lucinda John

Lucinda John

Lucinda John

Chapter One
Shanika St. Mark

"You are free to go," Sara, one of my favorite correctional officers said as she scribbled on some papers then slide them over for me to sign.

Accepting the pen, I licked my lips, signed each paper before placing the pen on the stack of papers then sliding them back over to her.

"Keep in touch and don't let me catch you back in here again," she winked, handing me her number, a bag of my personal items and my commissary check.

"Thank you so much, Sara," I mumbled with a smile.

If it wasn't for my eager urge to get the fuck from 'round this dusty ass place, filled with corrupted correctional officers and dumb bitches, I would've chopped it up with Sara, letting her know how much she meant to me. I despised these fucking walls. I didn't want to be suffocated between then longer than I had to, so that sentimental conversation was just going to have to be a reserved another day. I had Sara's number, so I planned to call once I got to where I was going.

"Here's a seven-day bus pass and a three-day hotel stay voucher for the motel a few blocks over. I know you have a nice chunk of change left over from your commissary, but I placed a couple of dollars in that envelope," Sara spoke in a hushed tone, while looking over her shoulder to make sure no one was watching.

"I appreciate you so much." I nodded for everything," I sincerely said.

The day I was processed, Sara had her cape on saving me. My first day in was one for the books. If I was a rapper my first day experience would be something I'd pen in a song. I ended up being locked up in the same cell as Alegra, a chick who I shared this nigga, Tommy with. Shit, running around Tommy was the reason I ended up catching a case anyways, so I wasn't even thinking about that nigga, I was done with his ass. None of that shit mattered to Alegra. She was still salty behind the way Tommy left her for dead after she got sentenced to eight years for taking a gun charge for him that she was out for my blood.

Alegra was fucking with Tommy before I was. When I met Tommy, it was only supposed to be on some get money type shit. Tommy was a scammer getting money and I was broke and hungry. I was young and desperate so when Tommy had me open all these bank accounts so he can process fake checks through them, I was game. Especially since I was getting paid one thousand per check. That wasn't shit compared to what Tommy was getting, but at the time I didn't have a pot to piss in or a window to throw it out of so I accepted every dollar I could get.

When I was unable to open any more bank accounts in my name, I started recruiting other girls and before I knew it the money train started tolling. Tommy took a liking to how determined I was in return he took me under his wing teaching me everything I knew. We instantly became work *husband and wife.* The whole hood knew that Tommy and Alegra were together, but looked at us as some ghetto, celebrity, power couple. One thing led to another, and I found myself face down ass up in a hotel room with Tommy's head between my booty checks eating the fuck out of my groceries. That Night Tommy had my head gone and I willingly entered a toxic ass love triangle.

It didn't take long for Alegra to find out that I was fucking her nigga. When she did all hell broke loose. Alegra knew that Tommy wouldn't stop fucking with me because together we were bringing in a lot of money, so whenever she saw me, it was on sight. Alegra and I fought in clubs, stores, hair salons, she even pulled up to my house a few times to throw hands. It was bad, but that didn't stop me from getting money with Tommy and fucking him in our downtime.

Me and Tommy relationship progressed when Alegra got pulled over riding around with Tommy's gun under her seat. Instead of snitching on him she took the charge thinking that would be the saving grace to their rocky relationship. Tommy made sure she had the best defense team and kept her books full, but slowly he started pulling away from her. The more money we got together and the more we fucked made it easier for Alegra to become a thing of the past. I became Tommy's bitch, and I was proud until we got knocked a year later.

At twenty- three I found myself facing check fraud chargers, because some bitch I put on got caught and started snitching. Since it was my first offense, my lawyers were able to get me two years behind bars with two-year probation. I didn't like the idea of being locked up just to be released and locked up again by having to piss in a cup and report to some slouchy ma'fucka every week, so I decided to do my entire four-year bid behind bars just so I could come home a free woman.

Tommy on the other hand was into some deeper shit. Along with the drug charges, he was linked to two murders. Even the best defense team couldn't get him off therefore he had no choice but to accept the hefty twenty-five-year prison sentence that ADA placed on the table. The day the judge sealed our fate shipping us off to different prison was the day our relationship ended putting an end to our run as the hood Bonnie and Clyde.

Alegra didn't give a fuck though. When I got locked into the same cell as her, she didn't say shit to me. She didn't when look my way. Naively I thought there was no beef until it was time to eat lunch. I didn't even get a chance to put my tray down on the table properly before I was ambushed by six bitches, Alegra being the leader of the pack. I tried to fight back, but I had a lot of big bitches on me making the task impossible.

When the guards finally pulled the girls of me, I was fighting for my life... literally. Alegra had stabbed me up a few times with handmade shank, leaving me on the floor for dead. If it wasn't for Sara quickly spraining into action, applying pressure to my wounds and rapidly getting me to the infirmary, I would've died. That day Sara saved my life.

Sara made it her personal mission to always make sure I was good, claiming that I reminded her of her daughter that she lost to domestic violence a few years ago. Aside from my cousin, Lisa, I didn't have anyone to help me through this prison bid, so I accepted all the love Sara was willing to give. Instantly she become my surrogate mother and I became a temporary replacement for the daughter she loss.

Gathering my items, I gave Sara a final smile before rushing out of the building.

The moment my tan jailhouse slippers touched the pavement I was able to exhale. When I learned that I was being released two weeks earlier for good behavior, I was anxious. Now that I was free, I didn't know what the fuck to do with myself. Gazing back at the building I sighed, for the last four years *Lowell Correctional Institution* was *home,* Sara was my mother and life... believe it or not was simple for me. Despite my hatred for the facility that had me caged up like an animal, I felt some sense of peace knowing that I had a day-to-day routine to stick to. Being thrust into the real world after being shielded from it for four years had me feeling uneasy. The further I walked away from the facility the more anxiety began to fill me.

Breathe.

Making three blocks to the hotel, I walked inside. The small, outdated wasn't much but it smelt like fresh berries. The cute, short, old black lady with salt and peppered colored curls looked up at me then smiled. Behind her stood an old black man with a bald, shiny head shuffling through paperwork while he hummed a song I wasn't familiar with.

"How can I help you, beautiful?" the lady asked as I approached the desk.

Inwardly I frowned. I knew there was nothing beautiful about my thick, bushy straight backs and jailhouse attire, but still I nodded and smiled.

"Umm..." I stated, fumbling with the voucher Sara gave me. "I—I have this," I stuttered handed it to her.

"Let's see here," she said, while adjusting her glasses that hung around her neck by a cord. "Looks like you got a three day stay with us." Placing the voucher down on the counter, she tapped on the keys of her computer before briefly looking up at me, then looking back down at the computer screen.

"Do you have your ID?" she questioned.

"Yes," I replied, handing it to her.

"Ok, looks like we got an available room for you," she spoke while tapping on the keys some more. "Here we go, room three- one- seven." Pulling a small envelop from underneath the desk, she scribbled the number of the room on it before slipping two keycards inside then handing it to me.

"Check out is at eleven, the wifi password is written on the envelop, and we offer free breakfast every morning from seven until eleven in the morning," she explained in a chipper tone while smacking on the peppermint she was sucking on.

"If you need anything feel free to ask." Her tone was warm letting me know that she was being genuine.

"Do you know where I can find a check cashing store?" I questioned, running my fingers along the edges of my check.

"Yes, there's one five blocks ahead," she said, her eyes landing on my bus pass.

"There's a bus stop around the corner that will take you there."

"Thank you so much," I sweetly spoke as I backed out of the office.

Since the hotel was only three floors high there were no elevator, so I had to walk up three flights of stairs to get to my room. I was no stranger to fitness, so I didn't mind. While I was incarcerated, we were required to run or walk daily as their way to promote physical health. Wish was stupid to me since the bullshit they served us to eat was anything but healthy. If it wasn't for Lisa holding it down by regularly putting money on my books, I would've starved.

Slipping the keycard into the door, a blinking light appeared signaling that the door was unlocked. Pushing the door open, I entered the cool outdated room. The green walls and pink floral décor reminded me of something you would see at your grandmother's house. The ugly brown carpet was recently vacuumed, in the center of the room was a neatly made king sized bed sitting across from an old, chipped TV stand with a grey flat screen TV on top of it. Despite how old the room looked, it was cleaned and an upgrade from the box I spent the last four years staying in.

Shedding the jailhouse gear from my body, I rushed to the bathroom to take a much needed, hot shower. Never in a million years did I think the ability to take a long, private shower would become a luxury. Scrubbing my body with the small hotel soap, I indulged in the feeling of the hot water beating against my tensed body until my skin wrinkled against the cold water. Stepping out of the shower, I wrapped myself with a large white towel then made my way in front of the massive window.

Dropping my towel, I twisted from side to side taking in my newly developed body. Don't get me wrong, I was a bad bitch four years ago when I got locked up, I just didn't have the body I did now. Back then, I was slim with enough booty to accentuate my shape, now I was Big Nika with a thick waist, wide hips, fat ass and the legs to match. Shit, with all that fucking time on my hand there wasn't shit to do but workout. I fucked around a stumbled across a fitness book in the library and started living by that ma'fucka as if it was the Bible. I kept my workout simple, but I made sure to focus on the important muscle groups, my ass, stomach, arms and legs. In no time I was walking around the prison yard as if there was a plastic surgeon on the facility handing out tummy tucks and BBLS.

Moisturizing my smooth, peanut butter colored skin with the lotion provided by the hotel, I used the deodorant that was supplied by them too. Stepping into a pair of jeans that were in the bag Sara handed me, I did the *wiggle, wiggle, hop, hop* dance in order to pull them over my ass before slipping the black TLC graphic t-shirt over my head. Frowning at my toes, I stepped into a pair of black flips flops, none of which belonged to me. The outfit was basic, but I was grateful for the simple clothes Sara provided me with.

Opening the envelop, Sara gave me, I pulled out the three hundred dollars that was tucked inside, I placed it in my back along with my eight-hundred-dollar commissary check. Placing the hotel keycard, bus pass and my ID in the other back pocket I walked towards the hotel's phone, contemplating calling Lisa and letting her know I was free. Instead, I walked out of hotel room and headed for the bus stop.

"Is there anything I can help you with?" The snobby white lady asked the moment her eyes landed on me.

I was in a woman clothing store browsing through their clearance rack when Molly decided to fuck with me.

"I'm just looking," I mumbled, shifting through the rack of clothes.

"Hmph!" she hunched her shoulders walking away from me over to two white girls who received the nicer version of her than I did.

"Bitch," I angrily snarled, while discreetly removing clothes from the rack, checking for sensors then stuffing them in my bookbag like the boosting pro I was.

I had every intention to buy something decent to wear, but when the bitch decided to come at me waving her, *I'm a racist* flag, I resorted to drastic measures. I decided to teach that bitch a lesson. While the store clerk laughed and giggles with *her* people, I filled my bag with five different outfits. Since she was so deep into her conversation, I was able to slip out of the store without her noticing me.

"Dumb ass hoe," I chuckled to myself, getting a kick out of the rush I got from shoplifting.

Once a criminal, always a fucking criminal. It didn't matter how long your prison stint was, that illegally way of living would forever be embedded in your blood. What you did with it was up to you but being in jail didn't automatically *fix* you.

Strolling down the street with a bookbag filled with stolen goods, I started to instantly feel like *that bitch.* Stopping in front of a salon, I decided it was time to feel how I felt. The sight of different women getting different services reminded me how much I loved to get dolled up. Being behind bars for so long had a way at chipping at my femineity. I was forced to be hard all the time, walking around with chipped nails, and rocking the Queen Latifa braids from the movie *Set It Off,* just so bitches wouldn't get the wrong idea and fuck with me. Prison life was tough.

"Hello, do you have an appointment?" I was asked the moment someone noticed my appearance.

"No, but I was hoping I could walk-in," I said, looking around to see if there were any available seats.

"What were you trying to get done?"

"A full set, pedicure, hair, eyebrows and lashes," I replied, scanning the price list, making sure I had enough money to cover my requested services.

I had about a thousand dollar in my bag and I wasn't trying to spend it all in one place.

"What did you want to do to your hair?" she asked, eyeing my thick tresses in awe.

Since I was a little girl, I've always had long, thick hair. I was the poster child of black girls being able to grow long hair and although my mane was praised I was sick of it. I hated maintaining it and honestly it was time for a change.

"I want to dye it and cut it off."

"Cut if off?" she gasped, her brows raising in shock.

"Yes, cut it off," I confirmed with a nod.

"You want to cut all this pretty hair off?" she asked in a confused tone, trying to figure out why I would want all this *pretty* hair gone.

"Can you cut it or not?" I snapped, feeling irritated. I didn't mean to snap on the poor girl, but she was asking too many fucking questions. If I wanted my hair cut, I wanted my fucking haircut.

"No, but Bru can do it, she's the short cut guru," she explained, pointing over to a plus sized beauty who was sweeping up the hair from her station.

"Follow me," she said, leading me over to Bru.

"Bru, do you have any appointments for the day?" she asked her.

"No, I'm taking walk-in now," Bru replied, sweeping up the hair into a dustpan then tossing it in the trash. "Why wassup?" Bru questioned, glancing over at me.

"This client wants her hair cut."

"Alright Tanya, I'll take care of her thank you."

"You're welcome," Tanya replied, before smiling at me then walking away.

"Do you know how you want your hair cut?" Bru asked, dusting her chair off then motioning for me to take a seat.

I was grateful she wasn't like Tanya's pushy ass and didn't question my decision.

"I want to go ginger and I was thinking a short pixie cut styled with soft curls. I do want my hair long enough to grip just in case I ever decide to get some braids," I explained.

"I gotchu," Bru spoke while typing a cape around my neck.

"How much will it be?" I questioned.

"One hundred and thirty dollars," she replied.

"Got it." I nodded for her to proceed.

When Bru twirled me around facing the mirror to see my hair, I fell in love. The curls framed my heart shaped face to perfection, bringing out my dark brown almond shaped eyes. I felt beautiful again.

"This cut was made for you and that color... girl, that color looks good on you!" Bru beamed, grinning at her skills.

"I think so too," I flashed an appreciative smile, happy that I went with my first mind to cut my hair off. "Thank you, again." Reaching in my bag, I paid Bru tipping her a twenty.

Getting out of Bru's seat, I made my way over to Brenda's chair who gave my nails a natural overlay, coating them with a marshmallow colored gel polish. In Dean's seat, I got best pedicure of my life. The way his strong hands massaged my small feet and thick legs had me falling in love with his ass. Dean's wife, Lucy, waxed my thick brows to perfection before applying a thick, full set of mink lashes to my eyelids. Shit, I wanted to marry her ass too, that how good sis had me feeling.

Three hundred dollars later, I was a brand new bitch with the attitude to match as I strutted my fine ass to the bus stop and headed back to my hotel to change into one of my stolen outfits.

*****

Walking the streets of Ocala, Florida was new to me. Outside of being incarcerated here, I knew nothing about this city. I was born and raised in Fort Lauderdale, Florida, *The East*, if you wanted to be exact, therefore this was uncharted territory for me.

Glancing down at the time on my phone I sighed, I had just got off the last bus of the night and being that I had no debit card there was no possible way for me to order an Uber to Lyft back to the hotel. Going with the flow, I stumbled into a strip club that charged a ten dollars entrance fee. After showing my ID and paying the fee, I was greeted by loud house music and colorful strobes lights. This wasn't the strip clubs back in my hood. For one, the stripper's barley had ass and they showed no pussy.

Taking a seat at the bar, I ordered myself a *Tequila Sunrise*. While I slow sipped on my drink, my eyes scanned the club in search of my next mark. After treating pampering myself, purchasing a new cell phone, paying the club fee and my drink, I was down to my last twenty dollars. That wasn't enough to pay for a bus ticket back home so I had no choice but to make some shit shake.

The more I observed the scene the more it registered that I was in a topless bar. Home of the ma'fuckas from the cooperate world. See, it was rare that you found CEO's, lawyers, doctors and any other ma'fucka with stature in one of those hood strip clubs that had ass and pussy on display like shoes on a sale's rack. That wasn't their style since these rich ass cooperate niggas like to keep their shit low key. This was like their little sanctuary a place to get away from their nagging ass wives and bad ass kids. There was a mixture of black and white men being *serviced* by their flat booty bitch of choice.

Sipping on my drink some more, my eyes landed on a cute middle aged black dude in the corner looking nervous. This was probably his first time at a place like this and he didn't know what to do. Finishing off my drink, I stood and allowed my bare ass to sway freely underneath my maxi dress as I made a beeline over to him.

"Hey baby, you having fun," I cooed, licking my lips.

I was standing dangerously close to him making him sweat. The sparkling gold band on his finger caught my attention, but I didn't care. Today I was giving his wife some get back, he had no business being in here no way. If he would've stayed his ass at home where he belonged then he wouldn't have fallen victim to my scheming ass.

"It's cool," he replied, clearing his throat.

"Just cool?" I scooted myself between his legs, wrapping my arms around his neck.

He instantly inhaled my sweet scent, licking his lips in approval. The body spray I purchased from Walmart wasn't much, but it smelt nice and would just have to do until I was able to get my hands on some real perfume.

"This is my first time here," he revealed what I already know.

"It's my first time here too," I gasped. "See we already have something in common," I smiled, playfully nudging him.

"I'm Stan," he greeted me with his hand out.

"I'm Candy," I replied, slowly sliding my hands into his then shaking it.

Everything about my moves were sexual. Shit, I hadn't had dick in four years and Stan wasn't bad looking. He lowkey reminded me of William Allen Young, the dude that played Frank Mitchell in the hit 90's show, *Moesha*. If his pocket was long Moesha's daddy could get it.

"Candy, I like that name."

"Thank you. Do you mind if I party with you?"

"Of course, be my guess," Stan mumbled while waving the waitress over to take our drink orders.

While Stan tossed back shots after shots, he began complaining about how his wife wasn't giving him any pussy. He told me that a colleague of his recommended this place and he was hoping to get lucky.

"How much?" he drunkenly asked.

"What do you mean?" I played dumb.

Stan was under the impression that I'd been drinking with him, but little did he know I had been tossing my shot into the ice bucket that the bottle service came in. I had a nice little buzz, but I was still sober.

"I'm so sorry!" he palmed his forehead. "I though... oh god. I'm so sorry," Stan groaned shaking his head. He was clearly embarrassed for mistaken me as a prostitute.

"I'm having a good time with you Stan, you don't have to pay me to *enjoy* you." I flirted.

"Are you sure?" he asked with a raised brow. "I'm—I'm willing to compensate you.

"I'm positive." I giggled at how gullible his ass was being. Stan was eating my act up and that's what I wanted.

"Do you want to get out of here? There's a hotel around the corner," Stan suggested, looking around as if his wife was going to pull up with a soccer mom van filled with kids and pop up on his ass.

"Sure, lead the way." I nodded, finishing the rest of my drink.

Stan stood, removed his wallet and paid the tab leaving a fifty-dollar tip behind. Tucking his wallet back into his pocket, Stan placed his hand on the small of my back then led me out of the club. A few blocks later we were at what looked like a high class *hoe motel*. Judging by the way each bombshell walked through the double glass door attached to the hip of a well- dressed patron, I knew what time it was.

"Do you mind paying for the room?" Stan asked handing me wad of cash.

Glancing down at the money in my palm, I smiled. The way this nigga was dotting his 'I's' and crossing his 'T's' made me feel like this wasn't his first rodeo. Stan's nervous act was just a sham. This nigga was been out here paying for pussy.

"You can keep the change," he said when I didn't move.

"Ok," I hunched my shoulders, before walking towards the check-in desk.

"Dillan," I said, reading the name on his nametag. "I need a room for the night, can you do that for me?" I asked the white, pimpled face boy that looked as if he was in his mid- twenties.

"For the night," Dillan mumbled to himself inputting my request into the computer.

"Ok, that'll be two hundred and eighty- seven dollars." Dillan looked up at me.

Shuffling through the bills, I gave Dillan three hundred dollars, waving off the change letting him know that he could keep it. Folding up the remaining twelve hundred dollars, I stuffed it in my bag. I knew Stan's suggestion for me to keep the change was a thoughtful gesture to compensate for him getting in my pants, but that wasn't enough. I needed more.

The moment the hotel's room door closed behind us, I was on Stan like white on rice. Crushing my lips against his, I slid my tongue in his mouth while I rub his dick through his pants. I was impressed. Stan dick was the longest, but it had enough girth to fill me up. The feeling of Stan's dick growing in my hand made my pussy wet.

"Do you have a condom," I mumbled against his lips.

"Yes," he groaned, reaching into his pocket and pulling a couple out.

This nigga.

Stan came prepared, then had the nerve to act like this was his first time cheating on his wife. Bull shit.

Sexily stripping out of my clothes, I gave Stan a show good enough to rival any bitch at that strip club he was at. When I was butt naked, I undressed him. Then used my mouth to slide the condom of his short, stubby dick. Pushing him back on the chair, I mounted him. Allowing the tip of his dick to tease my clit before placing him at my center then sliding down.

"Ooohhhh!" we both breathed out.

It had been four years since I been penetrated, and we both felt it. My pussy was so hot, wet and tight that I was sure if I rocked my hip the right way, I would be cumming in no time. Plopping one of my titties in his mouth, I wined my waist on his dick, leaning in so that his dick would rub my clit with every thrust.

"OH SHIT!" Stan growled, gripping my waist. His eyes rolled to the back of his head before falling back.

"CANDY! MY SWEET CANDY! MY GOSH THIS PUSSY IS SO GOOD!" he shouted at the top of his lungs.

"Damn!" I panted, my body shuddering at the feeling of my first orgasm ripping through my body.

Pausing my movements, I waited until my pussy stopped throbbing before resuming my movements .

"I'm about to cum... Oh! I'm about to cum!" Stan chanted.

"Hold on a lil longer for me daddy, let me get my second one off." I wheezed, tossing one of my legs over his shoulder so he could fuck me deeper. Pulling Stand hands between my legs, I placed two of his large fingers on my clit so he could rub on it.

"Ohhh!" Stan's mouth formed an 'O', his tongue falling out.

"Fuck me back Stan, make this pussy cream on that fat dick!" I nastily growled, swirling my hips in a circle motion getting the full pleasure from Stan's dick in me and fingers on my clit.

I could feel Stan's dick tightened in me. Stan was about to bust, but I didn't care since my orgasm was right around the corner. Gripping his dick tightly, I bounced wilding on Stan's dick until we were both crying out in pleasure.

"Damn!" placing my head against Stan's chest, I rode the wave of my orgasm.

"Oh my god!" he uttered a throaty groan, his mouth slightly curling into a lazy smile.

"That was good," Stan hissed.

"I got more of where that came from," I smirked, pecking his lips.

Taking it to the bed, I sat on Stan's face and made his ass drown on my pussy juices. Once I was done with that, I threw my ass on him while he fucked me from the back. Stan wasn't the best in bed, but he knew how to follow directions. Fucking Stan was like having my own personal sex slave, whatever I told his ass to do he happily did it. When he finally fell into a pussy induced coma, I made my move.

Quickly rushing to the bathroom, I gave myself a quick hoe bath before changing out of my dress and re-dressing in a pair of sweats and an oversized graphic t-shirt. Picking up Stan's wallet, I bypassed all the cash and grabbed all his debit cards. While Stan was nice and drunk, I got him to spill all his tea. I knew that he had been married to his wife Elise for fifteen years and together they share a thirteen-year-old son and a ten-year-old daughter. I knew their wedding date and the entire family birthday. Snapping a quick picture of his license, I made sure everything was back in order before slipping out of the room.

Discreetly making my way through the hotel doors, I smiled at the cards burning a hole in my pockets. Itching to bleed them dry. Retrieving a ball cap and sunglasses from my bag, I put them on before making my way to the nearest ATM.

Slipping the card into the slot, I typed in the month and day of Stan's wedding date then smiled when it worked. The daily withdraw limit was one thousand dollars, so that's what I took from each card. By the time I was done draining each card I had five thousand dollars, sixty- two hundred if you counted the cash Stan gave me. Walking away from the ATM, I cut up each card, tossing them in different garbage can. With a decent amount of money in my pocket my stay in Ocala was officially over.

*****

"You back, huh?" Fin greeted me with a hug.

Fin was a tech guy from Lil Haiti that Tommy introduced me to. If you needed burner phones, laptops, modems and access to the dark web Fin was your guy.

"I'm back like I never left," I replied, tightening my hold around Fin.

Fin was like a brother to me. He was the reason Lisa had money to put on my books.

"I would've visited but you know..." Fin paused, stepping back he looked at me then smiled.

"I already know." I nodded in agreement.

Fin who real name was Edward Sherman was real discreet with his shit. That nigga lived off the grid, behind his computer screen, with little to access to the outside world. Fin was scamming on federal level, so he limited the amount of people that had access to him. In order to work with the Wiz Kid, you had to be verified by a high level scammer. Thankfully Tommy plugged me in making it easy for me to link back up with my old friend.

"You back on yo' scamming shit, huh?" Fin chuckled.

"It's in my blood baby." I offered with a shrug.

"You sure about this Nika, you just did four years behind this shit," Fin spoke in a concerned tone.

"I did four years because I was sloppy with my shit, putting bitches on I had no business fucking with. All that shit about to change now, I'm working solo dolo now. Plus, this shit ain't for the long haul, I just need to make enough bread to get myself back on my feet. Ya feel me?"

"I feel you," Fin nodded. "What you need?"

"I need a labby, modem, a phone and untraceable access to the net. I also need a credit card maker and a card printer." I called off my order.

"Oh, shit you back on your grind for real. I can get everything to you, but I'mma need about a week."

"Good looking out," I said reaching in my bag for the cash. "How much I owe you?"

"Since you fresh out of jail, I'mma give you the family discount. Especially since you was solid enough to hold it down," Fin noted, showing his appreciating for me not snitching.

If I would've given Fin up, I would've skated on all charges. The FEDS were itching for the chance to burry a nigga like Fin, but I wasn't built like that. Going into this I knew the risk I was taking. To willingly do some illegally shit then snitch when you get caught up made you pussy and although I had one between my legs there wasn't anything pussy about me.

"I'mma charge you three bandos for everything," Fin said causing me to smile.

I was prepared to spend the entire six thousand I stole from Stan but the fact that I would be able to pocket half of that made me happy.

"Ouuu I love!" I squealed, peeling off three thousand dollars then handing it to him.

"I'll let you know where the meet up spot is," Fin said, handing me a burner phone.

"This phone is valid. You can handle all your business without a trace," he explained.

"Thank you, I'll get up with you later," I hugged Fin a final time before he pressed a button on his phone that unlocked the metal doors to the warehouse, we were in.

Like I said that nigga Fin was real legit with his shit. The warehouse was only a meet up spot to talk *business*. Fin had multiple spots scattered throughout South Florida that no one knew about. In fact, I had no idea of he was gay or straight, had a bitch or kids, shit, I didn't even know if the glasses he wore were prescription or just some prop this nigga used to look like a tech geek.

Before I could turn around to tell Fin something else, he was gone and the doors of the warehouse were already shut and locked.

"That damn Fin," I chuckled, making my way through the colorful streets of Little Haiti.

I wasn't from Miami but being in this part of the city made me appreciate my culture more. One every building were different murals of the Haitian people, our flag, and a bunch of other things that represented us.

Stopping at a nearby Haitian restaurant, I decided to get something to eat. The moment I pushed open the doors to *Piman Bouk Haitian Restaurant,* my mouth watered. The aroma that filled the air made the long line I waited in to place my order was worth it.

Fifteen minutes later, I was walking out of the restaurant with a white Styrofoam plate filled with rice and beans, oxtails, a side salad with a large order of Haitian macaroni and cheese. Excitement filled my bones as I thought about taking a seat at the colorful picnic tables outside to indulge in the fine Haitian cuisine. My excitement was short lived when a nigga arguing with his bitch bumped into me causing my food to fall on the floor.

"What the fuck?!" I angrily growled. Looking over at the pair with anger in my eyes.

"Girl it's just food, buy you another plate!" The bitch snapped.

"Oh, hell nah!" I threw up my set prepared to beat this bitch ass until the nigga she was with stopped me.

"Just chill," he said, his golds shining brightly in my face.

For a moment I was starstruck. Looking into this nigga dark eyes, my heart skipped a beat. The brown skinned, cutie was a dead ringer for the rapper Pooh Shiesty. If it wasn't for the Haitian flag that was tatted on the right side of his neck, I would've asked this nigga for his autograph. The sexy stranger was slim and looked to be about six foot tall as he towered over my short 5'4 frame.

Everything about this nigga screamed, *thug*. From the three diamonds chains linked around his neck, to the expensive threads and the butt of his gun sticking out of his fitted jeans that slightly sagged, displaying the band of his Versace boxers, I could tell he was a menace to society. His boss aurora screamed, danger and his charming, good, looks let it be known that he was a ladies' man.

"Shit miss lady, I'm sorry let me replace that for you," his deep voice filled my ears, pulling me out of the trance I was in.

The hint of weed and mint on his breath sent chills down my spine. This stranger had a bitch in a frenzy and I didn't even know this nigga from a can of paint.

"Haiti, I'm sure she's good!" The bitch he was with spoke, revealing his name.

Cutting my eyes at her, I couldn't hate the bitch was bad. Her proportions were crazy and shorty had the face to match. Laced in designer from head to toe, she was everything a nigga like Haiti would want in his bitch.

"Eliza, just chill man!" he barked at shorty, causing her to jump back like the love sick puppy she was.

"Yeah, Eliza listen to yo' massa!" I taunted her with a smirk.

"Aye, chill the fuck out, man! You want me to replace your food or not!" He snapped getting irritated.

I didn't know what the acronyms, *DCHB,* on his diamond chain stood for, but I was willing to bet my last dollar that he was affiliated to some gang. The iced out Haitian flag chain he wore with his name, *Haiti,* engraved with diamonds in the center went hard. He was a Zoe like me, but even him being a Haitian didn't excuse the fact that he was rude being rude as fuck. Glancing down at his Rolex and designer threads, I knew he could buy me everything on the menu if I asked him to, but my pride wouldn't allow me.

"Nah," I shook my head. "I don't want shit from you, I got my own money!" I snapped making my way to the back of the line.

"Man," Haiti drawled tugging on the small patch of hair under his chin.

Linking his arms around my waist, chills were sent though my spine. I wanted to object when he walked me to the front of the line, but I was at lost for words. The scent of his cologne temporarily left paralyzed me as I stood next to him listening to him recall my order. Pulling a thick wad of money from his pocket he paid for my food, then handed me a fifty for my troubles.

"I'll be seeing you," Haiti gazed down at me then smirked before walking out of the restaurant with his little puppy following closely behind him.

Chapter Two
Damos "Haiti" Pierre

"Haiti, I wanted something to eat," Eliza wined as we got in my car and pulled off.

"You should've thought about that shit before you started going off on shorty!" I snapped, cutting the car next to me off then speeding off.

"If you wasn't tryna give a nigga static over some shit that was above your paygrade then I wouldn't have bumped into her!"

"Fuck her! That ugly bitch was looking at you like she wanted to fuck or sumn'," she scoffed, her long nails tapping against her phone as she texted.

"Man, that girl wasn't ugly!" I waved Eliza off thinking about that fine ass stranger I bumped into.

There wasn't a lot of females that could pull of that bald headed look, but that hair style looked like it was made for her. Unlike Eliza, the way her ass and legs matched, shorty body looked like it was homegrown. I wasn't the type to fawn over a broad, but the mystery girl left me intrigued. If I ever caught up with shorty again, I was guaranteed to bend her ass over and put her slick mouth having ass in her place.

"You defending the bitch like you was checking for her." She put her phone down to side eye me.

"And if I was, that don't have shit to do with you! You keep tryna clock my move like we going steady or some shit!" I barked at her.

"You wasn't saying all that shit when you was between my legs!" she mumbled as if me giving he the dick she begged me for, made us a couple.

Me and Eliza had a long history of fucking around with each other. Growing up, Eliza and my little sister were practically joint at the hip. They started off in the sandbox and ended up graduating nursing school and becoming nurses, together. I never looked at Eliza that was until I was mourning the death of my fiancé two years ago.

Stacy was my high school sweetheart. She would help me bag up weed when I started off at the bottom as a corner boy and held it down when I started pushing pounds of Exotic for the Jamaicans. I didn't need a right because Stacy was that and more. If I was busting my gun, Stacy was right behind me busting her, no questions asked. She was a lot harder than a lot of these niggas out here which was why I decided to put a ring on it.

Shortly after our engagement, Stacy went out with her friends to celebrate. What was supposed to be a fun night ended in tragedy. The four friends decided to drive home drunk. Vickie, Stacy's best friend, who was also the driver ended up running off the road and into a lake. Sadly, all four girls' loss their life that tragic night. Every day I beat myself up for not being there. At the time I was in Jamacia meeting with my plug, Rasta. Had I been home I would've never allowed Vickie to drive them home drunk.

A week after putting Stacy in the ground, Eliza's mother passed away in a car crash. Experiencing the same tragic loss caused us to form a trauma bond. We were the only one who understood each other and from there a sexual relationship between us bloomed. Eliza wasn't the female I saw myself settling down with, shit, I told her ass straight up that I didn't see us being more than fuck buddies, she agreed.

I fucked bitches from time to time, but I made sure they all knew that no strings would be attached. Losing Stacy fucked me up so bad that I shut down. The thought of loving another broad that deep then losing her had a nigga swearing off relationships.

"I'm between the legs of a lot of different bitches! You not the only one I'm fucking!" I shook my head.

"Really Haiti?" Eliza gasped, as if what I was saying was news to her.

"You kill me with that shit," I grunted, licking my lips. Tugging on my beard, I looked over at Eliza then shook my head.

"You we're not in a relationship. You know I fuck other bitches. You know I'm not looking for love, just a quick nut. The fact that you know all this shit and still carrying on prove yo ass in delusional and maybe I should cool off yo ass!"

"You ain't gotta do all that," Eliza's voice trembled as she spoke.

"Nah cuz you been on some other shit for real! The last couple of times we fucked it was because you initiated that shit. Stop coming at me like I'm some gook as nigga, like I'm out here down bad over that lil pussy when you the one that can't leave this dick alone!"

"All I'm just saying is to respect my mind whenever I'm around," she smacked her lips.

"Respect your mind for what? I'M SINGLE!" I shouted, rubbing my temple to ease the instant headache I was getting.

"I know that but…"

"But nothing, man! I'mma just drop yo ass off at home, 'cause I ain't really tryna deal witcho shit right now."

"You might as well ride to yo parents house, Dina told me about your mom's party. I was on my way over there anyways," she huffed.

"Yeah ok, but you better make sure Dina bring yo ass home too 'cause, I ain't fucking witchu' nomo'!"

"You doing the most!" Eliza shrilled in a panicked tone.

"Oh, now you over there shaking in ya fucking boots," I chuckled. "The thought of me taking this dick away from you got you in shambles." I grabbed my dick then smirked.

It was something about that Zoe dick that drove the bitches crazy. Maybe it was because us Haitian niggas knew how to gouye, which was a dance movement the specialized in the slow, meticulous movement of the hips or maybe my dick was dipped in Voodoo or some shit. Whatever it was left every broad I gave this dick to stuck. I had a broad tell me once that fucking with me made her understand why fiends got addicted to dope. One hit of that good shit was liable to have any head gone. I laughed it off then, but now I was starting to believe that there was some truth to that shit.

"Please don't take it away," she pleaded with her eyes.

"Keep acting crazy and I will!" I replied, pulling into my parents' drive way the parking my car.

The moment my car came to a stop, Dina was opening the passenger door pulling Eliza in for a hug. Looking over at me, Dina mugged me before the pair walked away.

Shaking my head, I laughed. I knew Dina wouldn't be mad at me for long, she loved me too much. She loved Eliza too which was why she was against us fucking around. Dina knew what type of time I was on and didn't want to risk losing her longtime friend because I refused to commit, but Eliza assured her that she was a big girl.

"Big brother!" Carlie, my Irish twin rushed over to me, wrapping her arms around my waist.

"You know you fucked up by coming right?" she sighed.

"It's her birthday," I offered as an explanation.

"Give them some more time, Damos," Carlie tightened her arms around my waist, gazing up at me with pleading eyes.

"Carlene," I called her out by her government name since she wanted to refer to me by mine. "What I told you about that Damos bullshit?" I ruffled her hair, messing up her curls.

"Stop!" Carlie punched me in the side then stepped away from me. "You will always be Damos to me. Now run me my coins since you want to fuck my hair up and shit!" Carlie held her hands out.

"Whatever, man. You gon' always find a way to stick your hand in my pockets," I placed three hundred dollars in the palm of her hands. "I already got you on my payroll. I shouldn't be giving yo ass shit!" I jokingly snarled.

Being the oldest of the two; Carlie and Dina were my entire heart. There wasn't nothing I wouldn't do for them which is why I hustled day in and day night. My parents hated me for my life choices, they disowned me because of it.

My parents, Jonas and Magdala Pierre risked their life by traveling to America by boat when my mother learned she was pregnant with me. America offered opportunities that Haiti didn't so they had no choice to flee, even though the mission was deadly. It took them three long days with no food and water, to cross the US shores. A lot of the people on the boat died of dehydration, but it wasn't nothing the captain could do but dispose of their dead bodies in the blue seas.

Fortunate to make it to the US alive, my parents were able to work in the country as illegals. The only reason they wasn't sent back to the united states was because I was born on American soil. Legally I was a US Citizen and because of that my parents were able to obtain visas.

Shortly after I was born, my mother got pregnant with Carlene. Then a year later Dina. If it wasn't for my mother having to get a hysterectomy due to complications with her pregnancy with Dina, I knew there would've been more of us. Thankfully there wasn't because my parents were having a hard time caring for us.

Growing up, shit was so fucking rough that the five of us were all housed in a small box sized, one- bedroom apartment. The girls slept in the bedroom, while my parents sectioned off the living room with curtain making one side mine and the other theirs. We never owned new, nice things since my mom had a job at Good Will sorting through donations. My father worked two jobs and we still barley had enough to eat.

Sick of our living conditions, I started selling weed in the ninth grade. My strict Haitian parents were against me selling drugs, so they gave me a choice. I had the option to leave the streets alone or leave their house. Realizing that my sister deserved the best, I decided to leave their house. I wasn't too far though because there were nights my sisters would sneak me through their window so I could have a safe place to sleep. I still went to school and got my diploma thinking that would put me back in their good graces, but that wasn't enough. When I presented my parents with my diploma my father tore it and told me to leave his house or he would call the police on me, that still didn't stop me from loving them.

My parents were against the drug money that supported Carlene through law school and Dina through nursing school. My drug money also paid for the big house they were now living and hosting my mother's party in. Since Carlene made good money being my and a lot of other ma'fuckas that wasn't living right, criminal defense attorney and Dina was bringing in close to four hundred thousand dollars a year as a nurse manager, my parents was under the impression that my sister purchased their home when it was all me.

I didn't care too much for the credit though. I was just a real nigga doing whatever it took to take care of his family. Leaving the streets alone was a no go, so if I had to stand in the parking lot while my parents enjoyed their party then so be it.

"You want me to get you a plate of food?" Carlene asked pulling me from my thought.

"Mommy cooked?"

"You already know!"

"Yeah, bring me a plate and give her this," I handed Carlene a wrapped box.

Inside was a diamond neckless, a bracelet and the matching diamond studs.

"Should I take credit for this gift?" Carlene grinned.

"Go ahead, just make sure she gets it," I said before walking away.

"Damos," Carlene called out, halting my steps.

"They'll come around soon," she said, giving me an assuring smile.

*****

"What we doing for Haitian Flag day?" Ti Zoe, my right-hand man asked.

"Shit, ion' really know." I shrugged as we removed vacuumed sealed bags of weed from the coffee containers, they were shipped in.

Proving my loyalty to the Jamaicans had me in the league with the big dawgs. I was no longer on the block nickel and diming. I was selling my weed by the pound. I only fucked with weed though, since that dope shit was too competitive. A lot of niggas wanted to be the next Pablo Escobar, not realizing that there was money in the ganja.

Shit, instead of serving just dope fiends, I was serving the dope boys that supplied them. Everybody smoked weed and because that shit was starting to become legal, the dispensary was where the money resided. I did It all though. I sold weed illegally and legally it. Whether you had a marijuana card or just wanted to supply your hood, if your money was green, I was fucking witchu'. I wasn't opposed to getting my money on either side of the law.

"Shit, I heard Broward is where it's at," Ti Zoe spoke while taking each sealed bag of weed and stacking them in different piles.

Today was shipment day which also meant a lot of niggas would be receiving product.

"Word?" I raised a brow.

"Yeah." Ti Zoe confirmed.

"Bet. We can slide through. Let's handle this shit, first."

Once we had all the weed separated by buyers, we loaded up the whip then spun the block to drop off work and pick up money.

"These hoes outchea'," Ti Zoe noted as we posted up in our hood, vibing.

"Yeah, I see them." I nodded taking a swig of my Prestige.

Scooping up the dice, I shook them in my hand before tossing them against the wall then snapping my fingers.

"You nigga ain't fucking with my!" I boasted when I hit again.

"Come Haiti you breaking a nigga's pocket," Ted, a nigga affiliated with my crew, *Dade County Haitian Boyz,* better known DCHB, whined.

"Stop crying, nigga and getcho' money up!" I chuckled, finishing my bottle of beer then tossing it in the trash.

Deciding I was done taking all these niggas money, I picked up all my cash then stuffed it in my pockets.

"I'mma let you niggas make it," I smirked, taking a few steps away from the dice game to post up against the brick wall.

Scanning the block, my heart swelled. Despite the numerous reports of poverty in Little Haiti, I was impressed with my hood. DCHB made it our mission to look out for our community. Whether it was back to school give a ways, food distribution, or investing in youth centers to make sure our children had a safe place to play, we made it happen. I carried my street name, Haiti, with honor. I had different variations of the Haitian flag tatted on my neck, back and chest. I was proud to be a Haitian, period.

Chapter Three
Shanika St. Mark

"Bitch! BITCH! BIIIIIIIIIIIIITCH!" my cousin, Shalisa squealed the moment her eyes landed on me.

"Girl, you doing the most!" I chuckled, pulling her in for a hug since she was too stunned to move.

"What the fuck are you doing here? I was to make that trip to Ocala and pick you up!" Lisa said, stepping inside so I could walk inside the house.

"I got released early," I responded, deeply inhaling the savory aroma that filled the air.

Judging by the sounds of the pots my auntie, Madline, was in the kitchen doing her thing.

"Why didn't you tell me? I would've came and got you."

"No shade, but I needed a couple of days to get my mind right," I replied, hoping she would understand.

Glancing around my childhood home, everything pretty much looked the same. There was a French version on the Ten Commandments on the wall next to a collage of family photos. On the dining room table was a bouquet of plastic fruits, behind the dining room table stood a china with all the good dishes that we were forbidden to touch. The temperature in the home was still hot as fuck since my aunt didn't believe in utilizing the AC unit in the daytime. The only difference in the home was the new living room couches that didn't have plastic covering them. Other than that, my aunt's house was the typical Haitian home.

"Bitch! Look at you!" Lisa gasped, circling me as if I was a piece of merchandise, she was interested in buying.

"Oh no the fuck you didn't!" Lisa fingers ruffled my short curls. "You cut your hair!"

"Oh! Oh! Sak gen la? *What's going on here*?" My aunt asked, pushing through the beaded curtains that separated the kitchen from the living room.

"SHANIKA!" my aunt eyes widened before she rushed over to me, pulling me in for a tight hug.

Relaxing in my aunt's embrace, I allowed a few of my tears to fall.

"Mommy," I sniffled.
"Ki le ou lagey? *When did you get out?*" she questioned, pulling back to get a better look at me.

"Pa lontan. *Not long ago,*" I replied, not bothering to disclose the exact date I was released. I didn't want that smoke with my aunt.

"Kijan ou ye? *How are you?*" she asked touching my hair.

"Mwen Byen. *I'm good.*" I nodded.

"Bondye bon, li fé yo lage' ou pou anivèsè ou. *God os good he made them let you go in time for your birthday,*" my aunt said, revealing that today was my twenty- seventh birthday.

I'd been incarcerated for some many birthdays, that I no longer acknowledged the day.

"Today is your birthday and it's Haitian Flag Day too, oh yeah we turning up!" Lisa added with the wag of her tongue.

"I'm not in the mood to celebrate," I waved her off.

"I don't care what you in the mood to do, my sister, cousin, bestie is home, after being gone for four years, hell yeah we're celebrating this birthday and every other birthday you spent behind bars. Chile, I gotta make you a fly ass Haitian Flag Day fit," Lisa ranted, glancing down at the time on her phone.

"I think I can whip something up before we leave for the carnival," she said with a smile.

"Mwen byen kontan ou lakay, *I'm so happy you're home*." My aunt smiled at me.

"Mwen konta mwen lakay, mommy. *I'm happy to be home, mommy,*" I truthfully replied. Being free and home with my family felt good.

"I go cook for de party. I talk to you soon." My aunt flexed her English speaking skills. Even though it was broken, I was proud of her effort.

"Ok mommy!" I giggled, hugging then kissing her cheeks.

My aunt turned over her shoulder and smiled at me before prancing into the kitchen while thanking the lord that I was home free.

"They got mommy cooking for the carnival?" I asked Lisa, following down the hall.

"Yeah, but she not cooking for free. She's a vendor this year so she'll be selling plated," Lisa replied.

Before I got locked up, I participated in every Haitian Flag Day event, especially since it was my birthday too. Celebrating the creation of our flag was vital to us especially since we fought hard for our freedom from France. My aunt would never go for me sitting this Haitian Flag Day out, therefore I knew I had no choice but to participate.

"How is he doing?" I asked, stopping in my aunt's room glancing over at my uncle who peacefully laid in bed with his eyes closed.

"He has his days," Lisa mumbled with a sigh.

My uncle by marriage, Saul, was diagnosed with dementia seven years ago. The moment my uncle got sick. Shit got hard for us since he was the breadwinning. There were days we had to choose between eating or paying the bills. My aunt, Shalisa and I all got jobs but that still wasn't enough to cover all our bills and my uncle medical bills, so I stopped working and started scamming.

Glancing at my uncle a final time, I followed Lisa into our childhood room that now belonged to her and her two year old daughter, Asia.

"Where's Asia?" I asked plopping down on Lisa's queen size bed.

"She's with her daddy's peoples," Lisa spoke while pulling out her sewing machine.

"Get up so I can measure your thick ass."

Standing to my feet, I walked over to Lisa, holding my hands out so she could measure me.

My eyes scanned the room, taking in all the changes.

"There's more than enough room for the three of us," Lisa said as if she was reading my mind.

The two-bedroom house wasn't much, but it was the only thing my aunt and uncle owned, so they cherished it. I still remember the look of joy on my aunts face when she learned that I paid the house off.

"I'll only be here for a couple of days," I revealed.

"Where are you going?" Lisa questioned, her brows raising in confusion.

"I'm working on getting my own place."

"Girl, you just out. Where you going to find the money to... oh!" Lisa paused as if a light bulb had went off in her head.

"You back on your bullshit, I see," she scoffed.

Lisa was the type that always kept her hands cleaned and I respected her for that. She graduated from a fashion design school and made money selling personal pieces through her online boutique. Lisa was also well known for her custom wedding and prom dresses. *Sincerely, Lisa*, was a big deal in South Florida and it was only a matter of time before she blew up everywhere.

"I gotta do what I gotta do," I shrugged.

"Shanika—"

"Don't try to give me a pep talk because I already made up my mind. While I'm here I'mma keep my hands clean, so you don't have to worry about that."

"I'm not worried about *that*. I'm worried about you!" she stressed.

"Don't worry about me Lisa, I'm good. I promise."

"Ok." Lisa hunched her shoulders, deciding to let it go.

Once she had all my measurements, Lisa got busy at her workstation.

"You had a lot of orders this year?" I questioned, shuffling through the photos that were on the dresser.

"Girlllllll! Did I? I was so swamped I had to hire an assistant. It's all worth it though. I'm closer to my goal of opening my physical store."

"That's wassup," I mumbled gazing at the old photo of my mother and aunt.

My mom and aunt were victim of restavek which was a form of modern-day childhood slavery in Haiti. My grandparents couldn't afford to take care of them, so they sent my aunt and mother to a wealthy Haitian family under the impression that their girls would receive food, room and board and access to an education while performing odd jobs around the couple's house. What my grandparents didn't know was that their daughters were sold to a white man that sex trafficked them to the US.

My aunt was twenty-two and my mom was eighteen when they were finally able to escape their captures. Unable to go back home to Haiti my aunt sought refuge in my uncle, Saul. At the time he was a thirty-three-year-old US citizen that had no problem marrying my aunt and taking her and my sister in.

Shortly after my mother met my father and got pregnant with me. The moment my sperm donner found out she was pregnant he fled, leaving my aunt and uncle to care for my mother through her pregnancy. Unfortunately, my mother died during childbirth leaving me behind for my aunt and uncle to raise.

I was four-month-old when my aunt found out that she was pregnant with Lisa. My uncle started a landscaping business to support us while my aunt stayed home and raised two kids under the age of two. When I got older, my aunt was honest with me. She was very vocal about my mother and the hardship they had to endure.

"You look like her," Lisa said.

"Yeah," I sighed, placing the picture on the dresser with the others.

I had a great childhood, my aunt and uncle raised me as their daughter and in return I addressed them as *mommy and daddy,* but that didn't stop me from wondering what life I would've live if my mother was alive to raise me.
*****

Donning a body suit that Lisa made from the Haitian Flag with a pair of booty shorts that rode up my ass, displaying the Haitian Flag tattoo on my thigh. I completed my outfit with a pair of white Air Force Ones, with Haitian flags tied around both my ankles and another tucked in my back pocket. Lisa was dressed the same way except instead of shorts she wore a mini, denim skirt. Lisa's long red and blue box braids were pulled into a high ponytail, her edges laid to perfection.

Lisa and I looked more sisters than we did cousins. We had a lot of the same features except she was still on the slim side while I was a lot thicker.

Taking in the scenery of the carnival, I smiled proudly. Haitian music blasted from the speakers while everyone walked around dressed in the best Haitian gear. There were different food vendors posted on every block and gift shops for those who wanted to purchase Haitian inspired trinkets.

Falling in line next to Lisa, we marched behind our other fellow Haitians waving around our flags as we participated in the annual Haitian Flag Day parade, shutting the whole block down. People that wasn't participating in the activity stood off to the side recording the parade on their phones. Haiti made history being the first republic in the world to abolish slavery, we deserved this moment. We worked hard for this shit.

When night fell, it was time to turn the fuck up. Leaving the catholic church where the carnival was being held, Lisa and I pulled up to the Lauderhill Mall to partake in the ratchet festivities.

Tatted on my chest yes, I'm a zoe I never had a problem getting hoes...

I'mma Zoe, by Black Dada, blasted from one of the many cars that was parked in the mall parking lot.

"It's thick as fuck out here!" I said as we pushed through the crowd of people decked out in red and blue.

"The niggas are out too!" Lisa noted with a smile reading my mind.

Scanning the crowd, Lisa was right. There were shirtless niggas posted up against their candy painted cars, smoking, drinking and looking at the ass of every girl that walked passed them.

"This nigga," I grunted the moment my eyes landed on Haiti.

"Who?" Lisa asked spinning around so she could get a glimpse at whatever nigga I was talking about.

"Him," I nodded over at Haiti.

"Bitch, that Haiti! The leader of the DCHB! That nigga in number one on every bitch's hit list."

"What about yours?" I probed. Although Haiti was an arrogant ma'fucka, I couldn't help but to finger myself a time or two at the thought of his plump lips tugging on my clit.

If Lisa was checking for him, then I was going to dead all thoughts. I was a lot of things, but a bitch that fucked behind my bitch wasn't one of them.

"Hell nah! I use to fuck around with his homie, Ti Zoe before I got pregnant with Asia."

"Who is Ti Zoe?" I mumbled as I licked the blunt I was rolling closed.

"That the nigga with the bonks standing next to him."

Looking over at Ti Zoe, I nodded my head in approval. He was handsome, with a muscular, athletic built and golds in his mouth. I wasn't a fan of bonks, those thick dreads majority of the niggas in Miami rocked, but they looked good on Ti Zoe. Ti Zoe's thick dreads were neat and his lineup was fresh. I could see why Lisa use to fuck with him.

"What happened between y'all?" I interrogated, wanting to know all the tea.

"He had too many hoes. After a while fighting bitches get exhausting, so I thought it was best I stopped fucking with that nigga. It wasn't like I was in love with his ass anyways," she shrugged.

"I feel you," I mumbled with my eyes still glued to Haiti.

"What's your beef with Haiti tho'?"

It was now my turn to spill the tea.

"That arrogant ma'fucka was arguing with some bitch and he bumped into me dropping my fucking food," I said giving Lisa the summed up version of what took place.

"If you talking about Eliza, they not together. They just fuck."

"Shit, she was bucking at me like they were together."

"She bucked at you?" Lisa whirled her head around wanting all the smoke.

"Yeah, but that bitch wasn't 'bout that for real."

"Chile, Haiti always embarrassing that girl, but she refuses to stop fucking with him. That dick must be dipped in gold or some shit 'cause ain't no fucking way," Lisa shook her head, reaching for the blunt that was pinched between my fingers.

Handing her the blunt, I took a sip of the Patron and pineapple juice mix that was in my red cup. Peering over my cup, my eyes found its way to Haiti arrogant ass, again.

Clad in a crisp white tank top and a sagging pair of jean shorts, the butt of Haiti's gun was on full display letting these niggas know he was strapped and ready for whatever. A Haitian flag was wrapped around his forehead, another tossed over his shoulder. The golds in his mouth glistening as he rapped the words to the words to Kodak Black, *No Flockin'*.

"Bitch, you watching that nigga hard!" Lisa giggled, nudging me.

"Girl ain't nobody worried about that fool," I cleared my throat, diverting my eyes over to the girls that were standing on top of cars shaking their ass.

Every car was blasting different songs to match the different moods.

"Ouuu bitch you remember how we use to kill this dance back in the day!" Lisa shouted the moment *Woo Tang Wit It* by Dj Chipman started to play.

"We gotta fuck it up one time," Lisa tugged on my arms as she dropped into a squat.

"Nah, I'm good," I waved her off.

"Do it for the Vine!" she encouraged, quoting the viral video.

"I ain't gon' do it!" I called out, mimicking the little girl in the video.

Dropping down into a squat next to Lisa, we rocked our hips from side to side while swinging our arms, executing the popular Florida dance.

The vibe switched from Dj Chipman to King Posse a Haitian group. Their hit carnival song *Retounen,* loudly floated through the air grabbing everyone's attention. Haitian flags were proudly being waved in the air as we all jumped around singing along with the lyrics.

Jumping on the car where the song was being played from. I placed my hand on the hood while I wined my waist to the beat. When song said put your hands in the air, I locked my fingers behind my head and started popping my ass.

"Watch out! Watch out!" Lisa shouted the lyrics as she danced next to me.

"Welcome home, bitch and happy birthday!" Lisa called out, reminding me that today was my day to cut the fuck up.

Hitting a full split on the hood of the car, I made each booty cheeks jump to the beat before jumping off the car then bending over to clutch my ankles as I wobbled my ass.

"I see you," Haiti smirked, linking his arms around my waist while I wiggled my ass on his dick.

"You see me!" I locked back at him, sticking my tongue out, never missing the beat.

"That's how the fuck you do—"

POW! POW! POW!

The sounds of loud gun shots interrupted Lisa's though.

"Ahhh!" everyone screamed as they all scattered to safety.

Pulling his gun out, Haiti rushed behind whoever that was shooting letting off shots of his own.

POW! POW! POW!

More gunshots filled the air as a tramped of people rushed me.

POW!

A bullet hit me.

Chapter Four
Damos Haiti Pierre

"Pussy ass nigga!" I seethed, putting a bullet between the head of one of the niggas that decided to fuck up the vibe by shooting up the mall's parking lot.

"The other three nigga got away," Ti Zoe panted as he ran back over to me, starring down at the life I just took.

"That's Fendi, one of them Sunland niggas," I shook my head, before wiping my prints off the gun then placing it in a bag.

"Them yanks from Sunland always fucking with us!" Ti Zoe muttered.

Yanks, was a term we to refer to the Americans that didn't like Haitians. Ever since I could remember there was this ongoing beef between Haitians and Americans. When I was in school, every Haitian Flag Day the Americans that didn't like us would start this big brawl. Every year it became a thing.

"I knew I should've murked that nigga last years," I huffed, mad at myself for giving this nigga the chance to get at me.

Last year, Haitian Flag Day, Fendi tried to flex on me but ended up getting his ass stomped. I should've put a bullet between his head then, but I spared his life. Now his crew was gunning for me, so I had no choice but to take them all out.

"We gotta get out of here before the laws come," Ti Zoe urged me.

Kicking Fendi's dead body, I took off. Running towards my car until the cries from two woman caught my attention.

"Yo ain't that shorty you use to fuck with?" I asked to Ti Zoe.

"Lisa, yeah… that's her," Ti Zoe said as we rushed over to them.

"Help me get my cousin to the hospital she been shot!" Lisa hysterically cried.

Looking down at the shorty that was on the floor, my heart skipped a beat. The girl that's been on my mind since the day we crossed paths, was laying on the ground with what looked like a bullet graze.

"Ti Zoe, grab her I'mma get shorty," I said before bending down and scooping her in my arms.

"I got shot!" she mumbled in my arms.

"You gon' be straight, it's just a graze," I assured her while rushing towards my car.

"I'm not leaving without my cousin!" Lisa yelled out putting up a fight.

"We gotta split up, but we gon' meet up with them later," Ti Zoe said placing Lisa in his car.

Pulling off, Ti Zoe and I drove off in opposite directions. Even though I wasn't from Broward, I did business with a lot of niggas from here so my face in the county was gate. Pulling up to a twenty-four-hour clinic that was ran by this Haitian doctor hired by the local dope boys to treat them without the involvement of the police, I parked.

"You straight, but I'mma have this doctor check you out just to be on the safe side," I said, carrying her inside the clinic.

"My friend, Haiti, how can I help you?" the middle age doctor asked.

"Doctor Santil, she got grazed by a bullet. I need you to check her out for me," I replied.

"Ok, bring her back." He nodded.

Carrying her into one of the rooms, I sat her on the bed so that the doctor could check her leg out.

"Yes, it's just a graze." Doctor Santil confirmed.

"I'm going to clean your wound, dress it then give you something for pain," Doctor Santil said, making his way to the counter to grab everything he needed.

*****

"I'm good, the doctor just dressed my wounds and gave me something for pain," shorty spoke to her cousin on FaceTime.

"Some fucking birthday, huh?"

"Tell me about it," she sighed.

"Where you at now?" her cousin asked.

"I'm about to get dropped off, where you at?" she asked.

"Girl, this nigga Ti Zoe ain't tryna let me nbe. I might chill with hm for a lil bit. You gon' be straight?"

"Yeah she good," I called out interrupting their call.

Shorty looked over at me then rolled her eyes.

"That nigga talking for you now?" her cousin giggled.

"Girl, just a mess, but I'mma fuck witchu'."

"Alright, Nika. Talk to you later," her cousin cooed before ending their call.

"Nika, huh?" I spoke looking over at her.

Despite her disheveled look and the bandaged wrapped around her leg, shorty still looked good enough to eat.

"Shanika," she corrected me. "Nika is reserved for close friends and family only." She snapped.

"Shit, what if I'm tryna be a close friend," I flirted, licking my lips. Peeling my eyes from the road, I glanced down at the Haitian Flag etched on her right thigh then smiled.

"I don't need no new friends..." her eyes glanced out of the window. "I told you I stayed in Deep Side, where the fuck you going?" she sassed.

"It's hot for me on that side right now. I got a lil duck off spot we can chill at for a few hours."

"Them niggas were gunning for you, why?" Shanika questioned.

"Hell, if I know," I shrugged, changing the subject. "Today your birthday, huh?" I asked looking over at the time on the dash. There was only fifteen minutes left in the day, but it was still her day.

"Yup," she smacked her lips.

"Alright, let's turn up then," I grinned mischievously, pulling into the driveway of my Airbnb.

Airbnb's were the new wave. Hood niggas from all over were cleaning up their dirty money by purchasing properties and allowing ma'fuckas to stay in them for a fee. At first, I wasn't really fucking with it, but my sister Carlene insisted that I invested in a few properties. I currently had two homes and was in the process of purchasing more.

"Turn up how?" Shanika asked, following me into the house.

"I got a speaker, some weed and liquor... shit the possibilities are endless." I smirked, eyeing the way her fat ass fell out the bottom of her shorts.

Damn!

"Shit, might as well," she spoke while taking in the décor.

My sisters did their thing turning the three-bedroom three-bathroom home into the perfect vacation spot. The pool in the back made the home was perfect for parties.

Hooking up my phone to the Bluetooth speaker, I allowed Pandora to do its thing.

"You drink Henny?" I asked, holding up a new bottle.

"Yeah, but I was already on that white," she replied.

"Shit, it's your fucking birthday, turn up!" I encouraged with a smile.

Grabbing two glasses, I added ice to the cups before handing her one.

"How old did you turn?" I poured some Henny in my cup then drunk it straight. Shanika on the other hand mixed hers with Red Bull.

"Twenty- seven," she spoke in between sips.

Placing a gallon sized, Ziplock bag on the coffee table, I tossed a few packages of Dutch wraps next to it.

"You know how to roll?"

"Yes." She nodded.

"Roll up then."

Doing as she was told, Shanika reached for the weed and began breaking it down.

Taking a seat on the couch across from her, I silently admired how fine Shanika was. Shorty effortlessly exuded sex appeal. The way her tongue darted out of her mouth to seal the blunt close made my dick jump. Thoughts of bending her over, watching her fat ass jiggle while I fucked her from the back plagued my mind, making it impossible for me to think straight.

"You want a hit or not!" Shanika called out, pulling me away from my sexual thoughts.

"Oh shit, my bad,' I chuckled, pinching the blunt between my fingers then taking a hit. Exhaling, I took another. Then one more before passing it to her.

"Ouuu this my shit!" Shanika jumped up, bouncing her ass to *Home Body* by Lil Durk. With a cup of Henny in one hand and the blunt between her hips, she skillfully snaked her hips to her the beat.

Standing to my feet, I slide behind her while she did her thing.

"Dru sex, drug sex, yeah, yeah. Rich sex, rich sex, yeah, yeah. I know you nasty. She be touchin' on her own body," I mumbled the lyrics in her ears as she pressed her fat ass on my dick.

The sexual tension in the air was so thick that I whirled Shanika around just so I could kiss her. I wasn't into tongue kissing random bitches, but the feeling of her soft lips against mine had me breaking all my rules.

"Ummm..." she moaned as I sucked on her tongue while grouping her ass fat ass.

Pandora was on point with the music as the song switched from Lil Durk to *Privacy* by Chris Brown.

Helping Shakina out of her clothes I took the moment to appreciate her curves, before quickly undressing then taking a seat on the couch with Shanika straddling my lap.

Shanika's small hands found its way to my dick then started jacking it as our kisses got real nasty and sloppy.

"Oh shit," I groaned at the feeling of her small hands twirling around my hard dick. Lifting Shanika by her waist, I slid her down my shaft.

"Ouuu!" she cried out the moment I filled her up.

"Damn, you so fucking wet and tight," I hastily breathed out, while collecting my thoughts.

I was far from a minute man, but the vice grip Shanika's pussy had on my dick made it impossible not to bust prematurely.

Tucking her feet at my side, Shanika gripped the back of the couch as he rode my dick. Opening my mouth wide, I allowed her to spit in my mouth as we intensely made out. Tightening my hold on her waist, I rolled one of my nipples between my teeth before sucking on it.

"Oh daddy!" Shanika purred, throwing her head back, exposing her neck.

Sinking my teeth into her exposed flesh, I bit, sucked and kiss all over her neck while she rode my dick.

Flipping her over in the couch, I slapped her hard on the ass until her back was arched just the way I liked it.

"You better not run too!" I ordered, sliding my dick back in her.

The feeling of her wet walls sucking me in, had a nigga thinking with my dick and not my head. I knew I was fucking shorty raw, but I was already too deep in it to pull out and strap up.

Oh, shit daddy, keep fucking me like that!" her loud cries filled the room.

"Like this?" I grunted, spreading her ass cheek so I could go deeper.

"Yesss! Ouuu! Just like that!" she panted, throwing her ass back out me.

In awe, I stood back and watched shorty fuck me back. The sight of my creamed covered dick gliding in and out of her slippery, warm pussy had a nigga weak in the knees. When Shanika tightened her pussy muscles around my dick, I lost it.

Damn, what the fuck was this bitch doing to me?

"You fucking me back, huh?" I growled, spitting between the cracks of her ass before putting a finger in her butt. Gripping her neck with my other hand, I forced her to look back at me as I spat in her mouth before shoving my tongue down her throat.

"Oh shittttttttt!!" she cried out in bliss.

The wetter her pussy got, the further my finger traveled up her butt and the deeper my dick went.

"I can't take it, this is too fucking much!" she mumbled in a high pitch tone.

"Nah, you was throwing that ass back at me, keep that same energy and take this dick like a big girl, baby!" our eyes connected as I continued to drill her.

The moment her pussy contracted around my dick, I started filling her up with my nut. Together we rode the wave of our orgasms as I slowly pumped in and out of her while we engaged in sensual kisses until my balls were drained.

"Come suck yo' juices off my dick," I said smacking her ass.

Pulling away from me, Shanika grabbed my balls bringing my dick back to life as she licked up all her juices from my dick, as if it was a popsicle on a hot summer day.

"Yeah, I'mma have fun witcho' ass tonight," I grinned, gripping the back of her head while she topped me off.

Chapter Five
Shanika St. Mark

"Do you have all the required documents?" The lady working in the leasing office asked.

"Yup!" I nodded producing the three fake check stubs I created, along with my ID, the application and the fifty-dollar money order to cover the application fee."

"Thank you," she said, retrieving all my paperwork then looking them over.

I was so confident in my check stub making skills that I knew the faked documents looked legit. Thanks to Fin for coming though with everything I needed, I was back on my money making shit. For now, I was getting money by making check stubs and turning money into bitcoins. When I moved into my place, I planned on making fake ID's and fake credit cards to match so I could sell them as a packaged deal.

This time around I was moving more discreetly. I only operated through my burner phone under the alias Tiffany, and I didn't do face to face meet ups. All monies had to be paid through a mobile payment service before the pick-up location was disclosed. Like I said, I was on my shit this go around. Them crackas wasn't about to catch my ass slipping, again.

"Everything here looks legit, do you have the first, last and security deposit?" she asked.

"Yup, right here." I handed her the other money orders.

"Perfect," she pressed a few keys on her keyboard before getting up and heading towards the printer.

"This is your lease agreement, once you sign, I'll give you the keys and a we can do a walk through of the apartment."

"Thank you!" I accepted the pen, eagerly signing my name on every line.

Once I had my key in hand, I let out a sigh of relief. The walk through was quick, I pointed out a few imperfections in the two bedroom, two bathroom high rise apartment, that the leasing agent quickly scribbled down on a piece of paper. After going over all the rules and regulations, I was left in my twenty- three-hundred-dollar apartment to soak up the feeling of finally being free.

*****

"Bitch, ain't that Haiti over there?" Lisa said, pointing him out as he exited Dolce & Gabbana with a few bags in his hands.

Three weeks ago, that nigga slutted me out in the worse way before creeping out on me leaving money on the nightstand so I could call an Uber. I would never openly admit it, but that nigga had me fucked up. You couldn't put dick all in my stomach the way he did, suck and lick all over my body while exchanged bodily fluids then leave me hanging. Shit like that was how psycho bitches were created. I wasn't going to front, that one sexual encounter with Haiti had my mind gone.

"Yup that's his ugly ass,' I sucked my teeth, acting as if I didn't see him or that bitch Eliza prancing behind him.

Judging by the amount of designer bags in both of their hands, Haiti was in this ma'fucka blowing a check.

While he played me with a hundred dollar he was out here flexing his pockets ad he cashed out in Chanel, Louis Vuitton, Versace, Gucci and Ferragamo. The nerves of this nigga.

"This nigga got me fucked up!" I said a little too loud.

"Watchu' mean cuz?" Lisa turned and asked me, suspiciously eyeing me.

When she asked me about Haiti, I reduced what we shared to a one-night stand, never revealing that I was lowkey in my feelings.

"That nigga walking round here with a big bag and only gave me a hundred dollars, what the fuck type of shit is that!" I said.

It wasn't really about the money, I was getting that. It was more about the principal. I gave that nigga *Chanel* pussy and he had the audacity to tip me as if I was a waiter at a restaurant. Nah, that nigga was trying it.

"Bitch what the fuck are you talking about, you don't even need his money?" Lisa rolled her ass, while holding up the bags she was carrying.

The money was coming in quick, so to celebrate I decided to take Lisa on a luxurious shopping trip at the Bal Harbour Shops.

"I don't give a fuck, if he's going to cash out and that bitch then he's going to cash out on me too!" I snapped making a beeline towards where he and that Eliza hoe stood.

"Wassup, Haiti," I smirked, cutting in between them and facing him.

"Excuse me?!" Eliza shrieked.

"You're excused, hoe!" I snapped, before turning back to Haiti.

"What's good, ma?" he chuckled.

"Shit, you tell me. You out here blowing a bag on this hoe when I know my pussy way better than hers. I wanna go on a shopping spree too," I boldly spoke, inhaling the scent of his Baccarat Rouge cologne.

Haiti was looking so fucking good with his fresh haircut, shinning gold teeth and designer threads that I almost forgot that I was on a mission.

"I ain't blowing a bag on no hoe, everything she got she purchased herself," Haiti clarified.

Turning to face Eliza, I chuckled.

"Oh, you's a ditzy broad. How you go shopping with a nigga you fucking just to spend ya own bread?" I frowned.

Eliza was too fucking cute to be this fucking dumb. Granted Haiti's dick was good, the best dick I ever had—good, but good dick wouldn't have me out here splurging on myself when I knew my pussy was equally good.

"City Girls down, five thousand points," Lisa added, shaking her head.

"Right!!" I co-signed.

"Anyways," I focused my attention back on Haiti. "I saw a Chanel bag I wanted," I said.

"You got it," he said glancing down at my bags.

"I know I got it, but you gon' get it!" I smacked my lips before linking my arms around Haiti and pulling him into the Chanel store, leaving Eliza back there to sulk.

"Get yo bag then," Haiti chuckled, as he took a seat.

Instead of getting *a* bag, I got three. Haiti pulled out a black card then swiped it effortlessly.

"You done shopping?" He asked.

"Nope!" I beamed, dragging him from store to store.

Once my car was filled with all my newly purchased merchandise, I followed Haiti back to his car for a *smoke break.*

While Haiti puffed on his blunt, I pulled out his dick and started sucking it. I needed one last fixed before I controlled, alt, deleted this nigga from my memory.

"Shit!" his head fell back.

Squeezing his girth with my throat, Haiti dick thumped in my mouth before he coated my throat with his nut.

Spitting his cum back on his dick, I pushed my panties to the side then mounted him.

"Damn, you nasty as fuck," Haiti breathed out, gripping my waist.

Tossing a leg behind his head, I bounced up and down on his dick as if it was a pogo until I was nutting all over his dick and he was filling my center like a twinkie.

"Got damn, you were worth every dollar I spent!" Haiti groaned, as I slow grinded on his dick.

I wanted to go another round, but the ringing of his phone interrupted that.

"I gotta take this call," Haiti tapped my ass so I could get up.

Stuffing his dick back in his pants, he got out of the car to answer his call in private.

Luckily for me, that nigga fucked around and left his wallet in the center console of his car. Quickly snagging one of his many credit cards, I snapped a picture of his license before putting everything back in its place.

"You tryna roll to the crib with me?" Haiti stumbled back into the car and asked.

"Nah, I have shit to do, but I'mma fuck witchu'," I smirked, pushing open the car door.

"Take a nigga's number down," he urged with lust filled eyes.

Haiti wanted more pussy, shit, I wanted more dick too, but the nigga was now a lick. Maybe after I spent all his furnishing my entire apartment, I would revisit the thought of fucking him, until then his credit card was burning a hole in my pocket, and I was itching to run it up.

"Nah, I'm good. It was fun while it lasted, tho'," I pecked his lips a final time before strutting off with his cum running down my legs.

"Yo nasty as fuck!" Lisa joked the moment I got in the car and she pulled off.

"Call me what you want, but I bet you can't call me broke," I boasted, waving Haiti's credit card in the air.

"Oh you a bold hoe!"

"And is!"

"Be careful, that nigga ain't nothing nice. Them DCHB ain't wrapped too tight" Lisa warned.

"Girl, fuck him," I waved her off.

Chapter Six
Damos "Haiti" Pierre

"What the fuck?" I mumbled while reading the alert text from my credit card company.

At first, I thought that shit was a scam until I looked in my wallet and realized that credit card was missing.

"What's good my G?" Ti Zoe asked, looking over at me with low eyes.

We both had the munchies as we sat in one of my favorite Haitian restaurants eating Bouyon which was a Haitian, beef, soup.

"Somebody got my ass," I showed Ti Zoe the texted.

"Damn, them jwett niggas dun' gleeced yo' shit," Ti Zoe said, basically saying that the scammers in Miami had caught me slipping.

South Florida was the home of the scammers and or that reason I stayed on my shit. I made sure all my cards were protected against identify thief. I received an Alert every time a purchase over five thousand dollars was made. These particular purchases wasn't on me. In fact I hadn't used that card I blew a bag on Shanika.

"That bitch," I chuckled, shaking my head.

"What bitch?" he questioned, sinking his teeth into aa meaty oxtail then sucking the juices from his fingers.

"Shanika," I revealed, opening the credit company's app on my phone so I could review the purchases that were mad.

"You talking about Lisa's cousin?" Ti Zoe mumbled, in between chewing on his food.

"Yeah, that bitch!" I scoffed. "Hoe dun' boulé *(burned)* my card on furniture and shit," I said in disbelief.

I was lowkey impressed how shorty got my ass. She was slick with that shit too. Made a nigga drop twelve thousand dollars on her in Chanel, fucked me real good, then scammed me out of six thousand dollars. I should've known some shit was up when she refused to take my number or give me her. Lil mama was plotting on a nigga.

"Watchu' gon' do?" Ti Zoe questioned, gulping down his cup of Haitian lemonade.

"I'mma figure out where shorty rest her head, then pull up on her ass."
"Let me know and I'mma ride out witchu'," Ti Zoe mumbled down for whatever

That's why I rocked with him as my right hand, he was a shoot first ask questions later type of nigga. A quality every boss nigga should look for when it came to selecting his sidekick.

"I'mma handle this solo."

"Man, you ain't gon' do shit to that girl but get some pussy," Ti Zoe laughed. "Pussy whip ass nigga," he instigated.

"Mind ya business, fam." I waved him off, before picking up my spoon and finishing my soup.

I decided to approve all the charges and leaving the credit card active. I was going to let Shanika slip up and lead me right to her ass.

*****

"Damos, you got somebody pregnant?" Carlene asked.

"Man, this was what you wanted me to call you for?" I groaned, keeping my eyes focused on the apartment building Shanika lived in.

"Mommy called me and Dina over to the house because she saw a baby lizard on her door and swore one of us was finally giving her a grandbaby." Carlene laughed. "I'm not pregnant, neither is Dina so that leaves you."

"Mommy and her Haitian superstitions," I sucked my teeth.

In a Haitian household seeing a baby lizard in your home meant that someone close to you were expecting a baby.

"She been having dreams of herself rocking a baby too," Carlene added.

"That ain't got shit to do with me. I ain't got no bitches walking around here carrying my baby. Check me out though, I'm about to handle so shit but I'mma get up at you later."

"Let me find out." Was all Carlene said before disconnecting my call.

The sight of a Fed Ex truck pulling in front of the building Shanika lived in stole my attention. Getting out the car I creeped up on buddy.

"Yo you got any packages for Damos Pierre?" I asked.

The delivery truck driver looked at me, then down at the box that was in his hands.

"Yeah, I got about four boxes," he replied.

"Let me get them."

"Good looking out," he nodded before scanning the packages then handing them to me.

"The fuck she ordered," I grunted, carrying the boxes to the elevator. Thankfully the luxury apartments she lived in came with bellhop carts that residence could use.

"Do you have a guest pass?" the security guard posted at the front desk asked.

"Nah, I'm here to surprise my girl," I said showing him the boxes that lined the cart.

"All visitors must have a guest pass or I will have to call the resident and let them know you're here."

"Like I said, it's a surprise," I replied, placing three rolled up three-hundred-dollar bills underneath the clipboard that held the guest sign in list.

Nodding his head in approval, he scribbled my name on a guest pass then handed it to me.

"Good looking out." I nodded in appreciation before tucking the guest pass in my back pocket.

Glancing down at the boxes, I took note of the apartment number before riding the elevator to the second floor, stopping at apartment *263*. I placed the bellhop cart directly in front of the peep hole before knocking on the door and then stepping aside.

Five minutes later, I heard locks becoming undone before Shanika open the door donning booty shorts and a sports bra. Just as she prepared the close the door, I snuck my feet in the doorway, pushing my way in.

"You didn't think I was going to find out it was you scamming a nigga!" I barked, stepping in the apartment, looking around at all the furniture purchased with my money.

"You only found out because I wanted you too," she smirked. "I ain't new to this nigga, I'm true to this," she hunched her shoulders.

"The fuck you mean you *true to this*?"

"Exactly what I said, I was sloppy on purpose."

"Fuck all that shit, I'mma need you to run me all my money back!" I grunted with a scowl, shorty had me fucked up.

"Nope, but I'll give you your card back since you decided not to block it."

"You really playing in my face like I won't murk yo' thieving ass."

"Do it," she challenged, invading my personal space with the sweet smell of her perfume

"So... so... so, you a scammer?"

"Amongst other things," she replied with a smug look.

"Ain't this about a bitch!" I tugged on my beard and laughed.

Grabbing Shanika by the neck, I backed her into the wall before pulling out my gun and placing it under her neck.

"The only reason I ain't putting a bullet in ya head right now is because I got identity protection my cards and I can get everything you took, back, but don't get that shit confused with me being some simp ass nigga. Try that shit again and I won't hesitate to murk yo' ass!" I spoke between gritted teeth.

Shanika was visibly shook. I could feel her heart pumping at a dangerous rate. I outlined the side of her face with the nozzle of my gun enjoying the look of fear that was in her eyes before pulling back and tucking my gun in the small of my back.

"You done?" she sucked her teeth, putting on a front as if she was moments away from shitting on herself.

"Yeah, I'm done." My eyes pierced a hole into hers as we engaged in an intense stare off. Removing my ringing phone from my pocket, I silenced it, then placed it back in my pocket never taking my eyes off hers.

The loud knocks at her front door is what caused us to look away.

"I hope that's the fucking police!" she smacked her lips as she pranced over to the door.

Hot on her heels, I followed her.

"Hey, wassup?" she nervously mumbled through the crack of the door.

"Wassup, ma? You gon' let a nigga in or what?" a guy voice asked.

"I wish the fuck you would let a nigga up in this bitch!" I growled snatching the door open, revealing some bum ass nigga.

"Last time I checked, my name was on the lease!" Shanika sasses, snaking her head from side to side.

"And it's my fucking furniture in this bitch! Unless that nigga gon' be sitting on the fucking floor, he can't bring his ass up in here!"

"I thought you said you was single," the dude nervously spoke, his ass shifting from me to my gun that was now in my hand.

"I am single, he ain't no body," Shanika waved me off. "Let me get rid of him and I'mma call you back over, later." She smiled at the soft ass nigga that obviously wanted no smoke with me.

"Bring yo ass back over here if you want to and I'mma have something hot waiting on ya," I grilled his ass.

"It ain't even that serious, my dude!" the guy rose his both hands in the air to surrender.

"Move the fuck around then, pussy!" I angrily grunted, aiming my gun at the nigga's head with my finger brushing against the trigger.

"Look at that nigga run," I laughed as he took off down the hall with the speed of lightening. "That was the type of nigga you was gon' let fuck?" I turned to Shanika and asked.

"I wasn't trying to marry the nigga, I just wanted my ass ate," she hunched her shoulders before closing then locking the door.

"Since you ran him off, I guess I gotta fuck you," she let out an irritated breath.

"You act like fucking me is a bad thing," I chuckled, grabbing her by the neck then pecking her lips.

"Stop fronting like that pussy don't miss daddy," I groaned, slipping my hands in the bands of her shorts to play in her wetness.

"Talking shit and my pussy over here leaking for me," I arrogantly mumbled against her lips before pushing my tongue in her mouth.

"This your pussy?" Shanika asked, her eyes heavy with lust.

"That's what I said, unless you got some other nigga you want me to murk behind *my pussy*."

"Since it's *your* pussy, come feast on it," she whimpered.

Carrying Shanika over to the island, I sat her down, tore her shorts off, then started eating *my pussy*.

*****

Waking up in Shanika's comfortable ass bed after fucking until the wee hours of the night felt good. Shanika's girlie pad came equipped with good pussy, AC, fast Wi-Fi, a well-stocked refrigerator and access to every streaming service available plus cable. I could see myself pulling up with a spend a night bag and shit.

"Ayo Shanika where you at?" I asked, walking through the quiet home.

I checked the patio, bathroom, kitchen, living room but shorty was nowhere to be found. Walking into the guest bedroom, I checked there, still no sign of her. I was about to call her until I spotted light peeking underneath the guest bedroom, walk-in closet. Slowly opening the closet door, I spotted Shanika sitting at a table with a robe, creating fake credit cards. When Shanika told me she was a scammer, I didn't think she meant on this level. Shorty had the closet set up like a trap as she put in work bobbing her head to Chief Keef.

"What are you doing in here?" she asked, snapping me out of my thoughts.

"Damn, who the fuck are you?" I questioned, starring at her in amazement. I had never encountered a female hustling on the level of a nigga before.

"I'm the bitch minding her business, why you all in my space?" Shanika angrily snapped.

"Shit, I was looking for yo ass to see if you wanted to eat the dick up before I left. I ain't know you was Queen Jwett in this ma'fucka," I replied, referring to her as the queen of scamming.

"I handle mine." Shanika eyes went back to the credit card she was making.

"These ma'fuckas look real," I picked up a credit card and with the matching ID.

"You do all this shit on your own?" I probed.

"What you the feds? You wearing a wire nigga?" The tone in her voice was chilling as she side eyed me.

"Nah, never that. I'm just intrigued that's all.'

"To answer your question, yes I work on own and no I can't put you on!"

"I respect your hustle and all, but I ain't into scamming. That's all you lil mama," I mumbled in a serious tone.

"Good! Now, if you can excuse me, I got work to—" Shanika jumped out of her seat, then rushed into the guest bathroom to empty the contents that were in her stomach.

Standing in the bathroom doorway I watched her throw up with a perplex look plastered on my face. The fact that I hadn't wore a rubber since I started smashing shorty, rose my suspension. My mother being sure that a new addition was being added to our family had me thinking Shanika was pregnant with my baby.

"Aye you pregnant?" I finally found the courage to ask.

"Nah," she shook her head before standing to her feet and making her head to the sink to rinse her mouth out and wash her face.

"It's the Chinese food we ate last night," she mumbled avoiding eye contact.

"Are you sure?"

"I'm positive!"

"Alright, bet." I nodded, stepping to the side so Shanika could get back to work. That didn't stop the wheels in my head from spinning though. I decided to let the conversation got for now, if Shanika was pregnant that shit was going to come out sooner or later.

Chapter Seven
Shanika St. Mark

"Are you sure you want to do this?" Lisa asked looking over at me before reverting her attention back to the rode.

"Yeah," I softly replied, glancing down at my phone then ignoring Haiti's call.

"You don't sound too sure." Lisa slowed down at a yellow light, irritating the fuck out of me since she had more than enough time to make it before the light turned red.

"You know you could've made that light!" I snapped, I was pissed. My legs wildly bounced as I sat in the passenger seat gazing at the window. I wanted to cry, but instead I held it all in.

"Don't snap at me hoe, you could've drove! Shit! Mad at me because I'm not a NASCAR driver," Lisa ranted with the roll of her eyes.

Licking my lips, I pulled the corner of my lip into my mouth to prevent myself from saying something slick. I was in a terrible mood, and I didn't want to risk me and Lisa going blow for blow because of it. Ignoring another one of Haiti's called, I decided to keep my mouth closed for the rest of the drive.

Haiti: *Come see me.*

Sighing at his text, I clicked off the message thread. I didn't need a conversation with Haiti clouding my judgement. If I entertained Haiti, I was sure I would've been on my way to him instead of handling my business. That nigga had me dickmatized in the worse way.

"I'll be in the car waiting for you," Lisa mumbled as she drove past the group of people on the sidewalk, pulling into the secured clinic's parking lot.

My heart sank to the pit of my stomach the moment my eyes landed on the protestors outside of the abortion clinic. This was really happening. I suddenly started to feel uneasy about my decision as I walked past the group of ma'fuckas waving handmade signs, shouting out how wrong it was to kill an innocent baby. The sudden change of mind had nothing to do with the pro-life ma'fuckas, it just felt like a heavy choice to make now.

Entering the clinic through the side door, I scribbled my name on the sign in sheet then took a seat. Glancing around at all the women waiting for their name to be called, my heart thumped. I thought about texting Haiti and letting him know about the baby, but quickly removed those thoughts from my head.

What Haiti and I was doing was cute, we were fucked buddies who were very fond of each other but that was just about it. Yeah, that nigga was sniffing behind my pussy now, but a baby could change all that. Niggas were weird like that. They could be fucking you raw, nutting in you and shit, but the moment you tell them you're pregnant they switch up. I wasn't about to play myself like that though. I couldn't put myself in the position of having to potentially raising a baby alone.

"Shanika!" the nurse called me back.

After taking my vitals, speaking with the counselor and getting an ultrasound done, I was placed in a room to wait for the doctor. Laying back, I closed my eyes praying that I was making the right decision. At the moment, getting rid of this baby felt like the right choice to make, but I didn't know how I would feel after the procedure.

"I thought you wasn't pregnant," a deep voice with a slight accent angrily spoke.

I didn't have to open my eyes to know who it was. When Haiti was mad, that Haitian accent was very evident. That shit was sexy as fuck. There were times I would purposely get him mad just so I hear his accent.

"You ain't got shit to say?" Haiti asked, followed the click of a door.

Popping my eyes open, I noticed the locked door and deep scowl on his face.

"You ain't supposed to be in here! HIPPA, nigga! You're violating my rights right now!"

"Violating your rights?" he chuckled, inching towards me. Taking a seat in the chair appointed for the doctor, my eyes landed on the gun that was resting against his lap.

"You the one violating right now tryna kill my seed behind my back!" he seethed, pressing the button on the computer, revealing the ultrasound picture that I refused to look at.

Haiti gazed at the picture in awe, before his eyes grew dark.

"You really about to sit up here and let these ma'fuckas scrape my baby out of you?" he interrogated in a chilling tone.

A lot of ma'fuckas didn't scare me, but Haiti did. That nigga was crazy and he didn't give a fuck about consequences.

"My body, my decision," I mumbled, avoiding eye contact.

"Man, shut the fuck up with that bullshit! The moment you let me slide my dick in you raw, that became my body too!" he exhaled.

"Shanika we two grown ma'fuckas! I was nutting in you since day one! You knew what the fuck could happen, yet you never asked me to pull out or put a condom on!" he shouted, droplets of spit flying from the corner of his mouth.

"I was taking Plan Bs," I whispered in a childlike tone.

I was starting to feel like a child getting scolded by her parents.

"Plan Bs, huh?" he scoffed, shaking his head.

"So... so... so... why didn't you just tell me you were pregnant?"

"I don't know," I shrugged.

"You don't know?" he deeply exhaled. "Yo are you sure you're twenty- seven 'cause you acting like a fucking kids right now!

"Having a baby wasn't in the card for me right now! I just got home from doing a four-year bid, I'm just now getting back on my feet, I don't have the time to be nobody's single mama!" I burst into sobs.

I hated how emotionally this baby now had me.

"If you would've told me about the baby, I would've told yo' stupid ass that I planned on being there! There was no way I was going to walk this earth knowing that my flesh and blood was out there struggling. Ion' know what type of niggas you've been dealing with, but I ain't built like that shorty!"

"Well, I don't know what you want me to say," I said, never taking my eyes from the tan walls, covered with informational posters about abortions.

The tension in the air was thick.

"I ain't letting you kill my baby," Haiti finally said after ten minutes of silence.

There was a knock at the door, then the jiggling of the doorknob, but Haiti didn't budge.

"Anyway in there!" a voice called out from the other side of the door.

"You're going to jail," I stated.

"Ion' give a fuck about nun of that shit right now, you ain't killing my fucking baby!" he shouted gripping his gun.

"You can't force me to be a mother!"

"I ain't forcing you to do shit! Have my baby then give him or her to me. You can go about your fucking business after that for all I care, all I want is my seed." Haiti's accent was so thick that the only reason I was able to understand him was because I was Haitian too.

He was pissed.

"And if I don't keep the baby?"

"Shit, you won't live long enough to know!"

"So, you're going to kill me..."

"For killing my fucking seed. An eye for a fucking eye!" He seethed in a serious tone.

"I'm going to call the police!" the person said again, while banging on the door.

"Angel, do you have a key for this door?" the person asked.

"The law on the way, let me know what you're trying to do," Haiti said unfazed by the ruckus he was causing from the other end of the locked door.

"Let's go," I sighed.

Haiti stood then waited for me to climb off the bed, tucking his gun back in his pants he swung the door open. The doctor and two other staff members stood there with a shock expression written on their face, but Haiti didn't give a fuck. He simple pushed past them, with his hands placed on the small of my back, leading me towards the front of the clinic. He nodded at the lady at the front desk before walking me to my car.

"You can go home, now. I got it," he said to Lisa.

Ignoring Haiti's presence, Lisa looked up at me. "Cousin, you straight?" she asked me.

"Yeah, she straight!" Haiti answered for me.

"Nigga, you ain't my cousin therefore I ain't talking to you!" Lisa snapped back, holding her hand up to shut him up.

"Cousin, you good?"

"Yes, I'm good," I mumbled.

"Did you?"

"Nah, she ain't kill my fucking baby!" Haiti growled, the vein in the center of his forehead protruding.

"Who the fuck you think you talking to?" Lisa got out of the car ready to fight.

"I'm talking to yo ass! Why the fuck would you, a fucking mother, bring her ass here to get a fucking abortion!" Haiti shouted at her.

"Nah, simmer down when you talking to my cousin!" I added.

"Shanika is a grown ass fucking woman that is capable of making her own decisions! Right or wrong I'mma have my cousin's back and I don't give a fuck how a ma'fucka feel about it. Y'all niggas be killing me with that shit, think you can just tell a bitch to keep your baby, and everything is going to be ok. Y'all don't know the half that goes into carrying a baby, having it, then caring for that child! So, miss me with the bullshit, Haiti!"

I felt like I was in a fucking twilight zone watching my cousin and my baby daddy go at it.

"Man," Haiti drawled, palming his low fade. "I ain't even the type of nigga to be arguing with a broad. Shanika, come on man."

"If that nigga jump stupid, let me know and we can jump his ass!" Lisa said, while pulling me in for a hug then taking a few steps away from Haiti so we could have privacy.

"I'm happy you didn't go through with it, you didn't look you wanted to get rid of the baby, but I couldn't tell you what to do with your body. Just know, I got your back no matter what," she whispered in my ear.

"Thank you," I sniffled.

"Eww that baby got my bitch out here crying and shit, ion' like det," she joked.

"Bitch, fuck you!" I giggled, pushing her away from me. "I'mma call you later."

"Alright hoe." Lisa walked to the car and got in.

"Ion give a fuck who you affiliated with, about my cousin it's whatever!" Lisa smacked her lips, snaking her neck, while going off on Haiti.

"My bitch," I beamed.

"You co-signing her bullshit?" Haiti asked, leading me to his car.

"And is!" I got in the car, tucking my feet under me.

"You hungry?" Haiti asked, pulling off at the same time the cops were pulling in.

"I could eat," I replied, gazing at the side of Haiti's head. This ma'fucka was crazy, I was even crazier because the shit he pulled lowkey had my pussy wet.

"What?" he questioned, looking over at me.

"How did you know where I was at?"

"I put a tracker app on your phone," he nonchalantly replied.

"You did what?" I shrieked, grabbing my phone then scrolling through it.

"I had a feeling you was pregnant, so I put that app on your phone to see where yo' head was at," he said, placing a blunt to his lips then firing it up.

"Oh, shit!" he mumbled, before ashing the blunt then tucking it behind his ear.

"You fucking that bitch that work at the front desk in the abortion clinic?"

"Nah," he shook his head. "Money talks," Haiti mumbled then shrugged.

"Whatever," I sighed, looking through every app on my phone trying to figure out where the tracker was.

"I ain't taking that app off your phone until you have the baby, stop looking for it!" Haiti ordered.

I'll just have to get a new phone," I sucked my teeth.

"Play with me if you want to," he warned, before pulling into the parking lot of *Manje Lakay,* a Haitian restaurant.

Haiti got out of the car, before rushing over to my side and opening the door for me. Placing a protective hand on the small of my back, he opened the door then held it open for me.

"Chile, I guess you a goon and a gentleman," I smacked my lips.

"What you want from here?" Haiti asked, ignoring my comment.

"I don't know," I mumbled, scanning the menu. Everything sounded good and the aroma from wafting in the air didn't make my decision easier.

Shaking his head, Haiti stepped towards the counter to place out order.

"Ban mwen youn nan tout bagay, tanpri. *Give me one of everything, please,*" Haiti said to the older Haitian man taking the orders.

"Youn na tout bagay? *One of everything?*" the man asked.

"Wi, mèsi. *Yes, thank you,*" Haiti confirmed with a head nod.

"Dakò. *Okay.*" The man said, before heading to the back to call in the order.

Since Haiti was order a lot of food, he had to pay for it upfront. Once the three-hundred-dollar tab was paid, Haiti and I stepped outside to smoke his blunt.

"You really carrying my baby, huh?" he grinned, blowing a cloud of smoke into the air.

"I guess so," I muttered, scanning the block.

Scanning the block, my heart felt full. Even though I was a Broward girl the love I had for Little Haiti was real. The way the colorful area captured our culture through art was refreshing. From the array of fine Haitian cuisine, indie galleries, to the hip crowd, the city was a vibe.

Haitian music floated through the air as Haitian women traveled to different fruit stands shopping and carrying their purchased goods on their heads, while holding the hands of their little ones. The strength of Haitian woman was unmatched.

My mouth watered at the sight of the fine niggas posted up on the block, donning tank tops, sagging jeans and designer sneakers. If I wasn't pregnant with Haiti's baby, I would've spun the block to indulge in one of the goons from Little Haiti. It was something about those dreads rocking, gun totting, gold teeth wearing, Haitian goons that always left a bitch weak in the knees. In my opinion, Haitian men should come with warning labels. Don't get me wrong, Haitian men were very attentive, they love spending money on their woman and the kings of deep strokes, but they were also possessive and known to have a couple of families ducked off.

Falling for a Haitian nigga was like crossing dangerous waters. I hated that hoe I fell for Haiti too quick so soon, forever bounding us with a baby, nut the damage was already done. I just hoped that if things were to ever go left that I was strong enough to survive the heartbreak leaving Haiti alone would cause. Shit, I wasn't a fool. I was the type of bitch to leave, but I was going to ugly cry the entire.

"You so fucking pretty," Haiti said snapping me out of my thoughts.

Leaning against the brick wall with the vivacious painting of the Haitian flag etched on it, Haiti linked his arms around my waist then pulled me between his legs. Pressing his lips against my ear, he kissed it before sprinkling soft kisses down my neck. My body melted in his arms as I inhaled the potent smell of the weed he just smoke mixed in with the lingering smell of his cologne.

"I purposely put that baby in you so you would never be too far from a nigga," he mischievously chuckled.

"When I first saw you, I thought I just wanted to fuck but after fucking you in knew I wanted more. I had to take you out the game for nine months, sit you in the house somewhere to keep myself from going to jail for murder."

"For murder, huh?" I scoffed.

"Yeah, ion be on social media like that but when I do be on that ma'fucka I be seeing all them niggas all in yo comments and shit. I'm not stupid. I know yo cousin don't be the one blowing yo phone up when we together. You got all the niggas and I wasn't tryna share, so I marked you," he casually spoke as if this shit was cool.

"You basically trapped me?"

"I mean, if you would've asked me to put a condom on or pull out I would've, but you was letting me run up in you raw, nutting all in them walls, so I capitalized off that shit, locking you in for life," he smirked.

"You so fucking weird," I cut my eyes at him.

"You fucking with my weird ass though, so what that say about you?" Haiti palmed my ass, before pecking my lips.

"I see you Haiti, you out here boo'd up and shit," some random nigga on a bike said.

"I'm on my Ella Mai shit, nigga," Haiti chuckled, before badly singing the chorus of *Boo'd Up* in my ear, butchering the fuck out of the song.

Chapter Eight
Shanika St. Mark

The clicking sounds of guns being loaded caused me to stir out of my sleep. Rubbing my eyes, I glanced down at the time in my phone before sitting up with my back pressed against the plush headboard. When Haiti insisted that I stayed with him during my pregnancy, I forced him to get rid of his hard ass bed and replace it with something more comfortable. Hell, I made him rearrange his entire house to accommodate me since he wanted to relocate me and shit.

Haiti stood in the middle of the room donning a black t-shirt, black jeans, with a pair of black combat boots on his feet. His back was facing me as he tucked a gun in the small of his back and another on his hip.

"I'm coming," he lowly mumbling on the phone as he pulled a black hoodie over his head before placing a gun in each pocket.

When Haiti turned to face me, our eyes met. Silence lingered the room as we stood there staring at each other.

"Where are you going?" I asked, breaking the silence.

Stepping into my personal space, Haiti placed his hands on the bed then dipped his head to kiss me forehead. He smiled, then pecked the bridge of my nose, my lips then the side of my neck.

"I'm about to handle some shit, I'll be home in a little bit," he responded, cuffing my baby bump he rubbed my belly.

Last week we found out we were having a little boy and Haiti was filled with joy.

"My lil nigga," he whispered to my belly then kissed.

"That's not what I asked." I eyed him intensely, as he sprinkled light kisses all over my smooth belly.

Thanks to the *Lwil Maskriti,* my aunt gave me, which was basically a Haitian version of Castor Oil my stomach was free of any stretch marks or imperfections.

"Lil man, tell your OG to chill on a nigga," he chuckled against my belly as he spoke.

"Duke, tell ya daddy to respect my fucking mind!" I snapped back, cutting my eyes at him.

"Aye watch yo mouth when you talking to my son." Haiti protectively warned.

The baby wasn't due for another four months and he was already spoiled rotten by his daddy. Although we hadn't discussed after birth living arrangements, Haiti filled one of his spare bedrooms with baby items. At this point, we didn't even need a baby shower, Duke had everything he needed plus a whole bunch of shit he didn't.

"Damos Pierre stop fucking playing with me and tell me where the fuck you going!" I angrily gritted, gripping his chin so he could see the seriousness in my eyes.

I was freaking the fuck out.

"The less you know the better." Haiti stood, kissed my lips then backpaddled from the bed. He winked at me then turned towards the door.

"If you walk out that door without telling where the fuck you're going, I won't be here when you get back!"

"Where the fuck you think you going at two in the morning while carrying my fucking baby?"

"Home!" I pursed my lips, crossing my arms over my chest.

"Alright, play with me if you want to."

"Nah, play with *me* if you want to."

"Come on baby, why you stressing a nigga?" Haiti heavily sighed, palming his forehead. Making a fist against the wall, he lightly tapped the wall.

"You dragged me out of that abortion clinic a few months ago, begged me to keep your baby, claiming you was going to be here for us. This shit right here..." I wagged my fingers up and down at his all black attire.

"Ain't gon' work for me."

"You knew the type of nigga I was when you first let me put my dick in you!"

"And I get that, but I'm more than some bitch you're fucking! I'm the mother of your child therefore, I deserve an answer when I ask a question."

Haiti chuckled.

"The less you know is better." Was all he said before ambling out of the room.

A few minutes later I heard the activation of the security alarm before the front door was closed then locked.

"Stupid ass nigga," I mumbled as I stood to my feet allowing the blanket to fall from my naked body.

Cum from the sex session that put me to sleep oozed from my center, dripping down my legs as I made my way to the bathroom.

I tried to use a warm bath to ease my mind, but that didn't stop me from thinking about Haiti. I wasn't new to this hood shit. I was aware of what Haiti was getting ready to do I just didn't want the consequences of his actions affecting our family. The thought of having to raise Duke without Haiti made me panic.

Stepping out of the tub, I dried off, slipped my arms through one of Haiti's Versace robes, before shuffling around the house in a pair of Haiti Versace slippers that were too big for my tiny feet. Slipping my phone in my pocket I made my way downstairs for a snack. Opening the refrigerator, I smiled. Haiti made sure the house stayed stocked with everything I craved. Reaching for bowl of fruit that Haiti personally peeled and chopped himself, I grabbed a Snapple Apple then sat at the island to enjoy my snack while scrolling through my phone.

Haiti: *Stay yo ass put! I'll be home soon with some wings. I'll even bring you a soda.*

Instead of texting back, I enjoyed my fruit while getting my daily dose of social media tea.

Once I devoured the entire bowl of fruits, I doubled back for another snack. Munching on Lays Potato Chips and pickled, I did a little dancey dance when I realized I had everything I needed to make some spaghetti. At three in the morning, I stood in the kitchen shimming my shoulders as I browned ground beef, mixing the season meat with spaghetti sauce then topping it with noodles and a dallop of Ranch.

I was in heaven.

After my meal, I started to feel heavy, so I took a nap expecting to see Haiti with my wings and soda when I woke up.

*****

"Where the fuck is this nigga at?" I grunted, while calling Haiti again.

It was now three in the afternoon, the next day and I have yet to hear from Haiti. An array of emotions consumed me as I called him back-to-back trying to figure out where the fuck he was at. Anger surged through my vein then was replaced with sadness. I wanted to kill Haiti, but I needed to make sure that nigga was ok first.

"He's probably on the block with his boys," Lisa said through the phone.

To keep myself from going crazy, I called Lisa.

"I don't know," I mumbled, tapping on the keys on my computer. My mind was so gone I couldn't even focus on the orders that I had to fulfill and drop off today.

"I'm sure if something bad happened to that nigga, one of the members from DCHB would've." She spoke in an assuring tone. Lisa was trying to do everything in her power to ease my mind, but nothing was working. I was worried.

"Lisa I don't want to raise my baby alone," I sobbed.

Fucking pregnancy and these damn emotions.

"You won't have to. I'm sure at any given moment, Haiti is going to walk through that door with a big bottle of Coca Cola and a pack of peanut M&Ms he might even bring you some fried fish." Lisa said over Asia loud singing.

Asia spent the last hour I was on the phone with Lisa, loudly singing along to *Gracie's Croner* on Netflix. I wasn't going to lie some of the songs on there was a bop.

"If that nigga come through that door alive, he's walking out this bitch dead!"

"Well how the fuck he gon' do that?" Lisa giggled. "I ain't never heard of a dead person walking." she continued to laugh.

"The Walking Dead, bitch, you ain't know!" I said, letting out a few chuckles of my own.

"Can you call Ti Zoe for me?" I asked, tucking the corner of my lip in my mouth while I waited for her answer.

"Oh, bitch. Hell to the fuck no!" Lisa shouted. I didn't have to see her to figure out that her face was screwed into a *bitch, you got me fucked up,* scowl.

"I mean, I ain't saying to fuck the nigga. Just act like you tryna see him so he'll tell you where he's at."

"Shanika," she drawled exhaling a deep sigh.

"Shalisa." I mumbled back.

"Bitch!" Lisa huffed.

She was dead set against talking to Ti Zoe, again. That night of my birthday when we separated, she fucked Ti Zoe. A few days later we had to jump his baby mama because she decided to pull up to Lisa's house while Asia was there. After that day, Lisa decided to leave Ti Zoe in her past where he belonged.

"Please," I begged. "I just want to make sure my baby daddy is alive." I partially told the truth.

I was hoping that Ti Zoe disclosed their location so I could pop up on his ass.

"Girl, you fucking owe me!" Lisa blew out a deep breath.

"I gotchu', for real," I honestly replied.

I really did have her. To show Lisa my appreciation for having my back, I planned on giving her the startup money for her boutique. Business was booming for me and the money was rolling in, so it was only right.

"Don't ask me to do this shit nomo', now out your phone on mute!" before I could reply, Lisa clicked over.

"Yo baby what's good?" I heard Ti Zoe beamed into the phone. That nigga was so fond of Lisa, but he was willing to do just about anything for her but leave his hoes alone.

"Wassup, bae?" she cooed in a fake tone. I was cracking the fuck up because I knew Lisa was over there gagging.

"Nun' just on the block cooling it with my niggas, you tryna pull up on me?" his hoe ass asked, taking the bait.

Niggas and females loudly talking could be heard in Ti Zoe's background. I strained my ears listening for Haiti, but I couldn't pick his voice out. Even if Haiti wasn't there with him, I knew his ass was alive. Ti Zoe would've never been so clam if something happened to his best friend.

"You sound real busy. I ain't really trying to be on the bloc around all them niggas right now." Lisa said.

"Man, it ain't even a lot of niggas over here. Pull up on me! If you don't like the vibe we can leave," Ti Zoe suggested, he was doing everything in his power to get some pussy out of Lisa. Unfortunately for him, it would be a cold day in hell before that happened.

Lisa didn't play with a lot of things, but Asia was one of them. Ti Zoe got placed on her *shit list* the moment her daughter's safety was compromised.

"Alright, I'mma pull up. Send me the location."

"Bet," Ti Zoe grinned into the phone before Lisa ended the call. Lisa sent me the location then called me back.

"Thank you, bitch!" I answered. I was already on my feet and on my way to the closet to get dressed.

"What you about to do?" Lisa questioned.

"I'm about to take my ass home, this nigga got me fucked up!" I lied. If I would've told Lisa that I planned on pulling up, she would've insisted she came with me. This was some shit I needed to handle alone.

"Call me when you get there, so me and Asia can come by and keep you company,' she offered.

I hated lying to her, so I made a mental to do some major ass kissing with another shopping trip.

Alright, boo talk to you later," I said before our call ended.

Grabbing a duffle bag, I packed all my *work* supplies and some clothes. I have every intention on taking my ass home after giving Haiti a piece of my mind. Slipping into a black Adidas sweat suit, I laced up my black pair of *beat a bitch ass* Air Force Ones. Haiti wasn't the only one that could get dressed in all black.

Chapter Nine
Damos "Haiti" Pierre

Placing a blunt to my lips, I deeply inhaled the *Purple Haze* that filled the center of the Dutch Wrap while bobbing my head to the music. I was in my zone. Last night DCHB went on a murder spree, taking every nigga affiliated to Fendi out, now I was clearing my mind. I knew the moment I went home it'd be World War III, but I couldn't risk transferring my energy to Shanika stressing my baby out, so I decided to fall off the grid until I was in a better head space.

Killing Fedi's and them other yanks was a non-negotiable, especially since I now had a baby on the way. Shanika would always complain about me keeping her in the house, but that was only for her and my son's protection. I kept a tight lipped about Shanika's pregnancy, to avoid them from being a target. Now that the nigga's gunning for me were gone, I could breathe easy through the rest of Shanika's pregnancy.

"Why you sitting over here by yourself?" Eliza asked, taking a seat on my lap.

Pushing her off, I stood then sat on the opposite side of the couch. I hadn't touched Eliza since I found out Shanika was pregnant, and I planned on keeping that way. I'd rather fuck a new bitch than to double back to Eliza delusional ass.

"Damn it's like that, daddy?" she frowned, placing her hand against her chest.

"I told you I wasn't fucking witchu' nomo.' I blew a cloud of smoke her way, before taking another pull. The effects of the potent weed had me way calmer than I intended to be, but I meant every word.

"You always say you not fucking with me nomo," she chuckled, waving me off.

"I mean that shit now and that's on Stacy!" I said, glancing down at Stacy's name etched on my forearm, a memorial piece I got a couple of months after her death.

"Why the sudden change?" she questioned with a scowl.

"I got a baby on the way," I revealed. Now that those Yanks were the least of my worries, I had no problem announcing the arrival of my baby boy.

"A baby?" she gasped, twisting up her face as if there was a foul smell in the air.

"Yup a baby." I nodded then smile. The thought of my baby growing in Shanika's womb brought my life a sense of purpose.

I was proud.

"So... so... so... let me get this right," Eliza paused to gather her thoughts. "You let me get rid of my baby just so you can turn around and get another bitch pregnant?"

"The fuck you mean *let?* Eliza you a grown ass woman! You got rid of that baby on your own. Don't put that shit on me!"

"I got rid of *our* baby because you wouldn't leave the streets alone. I told you to choose between us and the streets and you chose the fucking streets! You didn't fight for our baby! You didn't even show any emotion when I told you about the abortion!" Eliza shouted loud enough to grab the attention of a few of my crew members.

I never expressed it, but Eliza getting rid of our baby stung. When she told me she was pregnant, I was prepared to handle my business. Then she started pushing me to leave the streets alone. Pressuring me into a relationship with her, so I had to draw the line. I told her I wasn't ready to leave the game and I didn't want to be with her, but I'mma come through for my baby no matter what. To be spiteful, Eliza got rid of the baby.

When Eliza told me about the abortion, I shrugged it off, but deep down I was hurt. Despite Eliza scheming ways, I made sure to wrap my dick up every time we fucked. I wasn't going to risk the mistake of getting her pregnant again. I couldn't fantom the thought of losing two babies. That's why I was so against Shanika getting rid of my seed.

Reverting my attention back to the annoying ass conversation I was having with Eliza, I took another hard pull of my blunt, blew it out, then took another.

"You got rid of that baby because you couldn't use it to bait me into succumbing to your demands. Man, get the fuck out my face with that bullshit!" I grunted.

"So, this what we're doing now?" Shanika lashed out before running up on me and smacking me.

"Nigga I'm at home, pregnant with your baby, stressing over you well-being and yo ass over here hugged up with this bitch!" she shrieked in a high pitch tone before pulling her hand back and smacking me again.

Standing to my feet, I grabbed her by the wrists, twisting them behind her back before backing her into a wall.

"Just chill," I gently mumbled.

"Just chill? Just chill?! JUST CHILL!!! Nigga, you got me fucked up!" I could feel the heat radiating from her body as her chest rapidly rose then fell.

"Come on Nika, you gon' stress my baby out doing the most." I pleaded for her to stop. I'd become fond of having a son. I would be devastated if something was to happen to my lil nigga.

"You wasn't thinking about *my* baby when you left me at your house for a whole day to lay up with a bitch. You know what, fuck you! Me and my baby don't need you!" she angrily spewed, cutting her eyes at Eliza.

"Let me go so you can get back to that sad ass bitch!" Shanika struggled to free herself from my grasp.

"You on one shorty. You got me fucked up if you think I'm about to let you write me out of my son's life because your feelings hurt!"

"My feelings hurt, huh?" she sinisterly chuckled licking her lips. "Yeah, ok let me go."

Placing my hand around Shanika's throat, she gasped. I pushed her head back then sank my teeth into her neck until a soft whimper blew though her mouth.

"Ahhh!" she cried out in pain.

Licking the bite mark, I sucked on it creating a big purple bruise.

"Why you playing with me?" I gazed down at her through low eyes, bending my head to kiss her lips.

"Why you stressing my baby out?" I touched her belly.

"How many times he moved today?" I continued to asked, while I kissed all over her.

I didn't give a fuck that I was displaying affection in a room full of niggas that only saw the goon in me. I was still the savage that caught four bodies in one night, but right now I was on my R&B nigga type shit. Shanika was my kryptonite. She had the ability to have me doing shit that was out of the ordinary.

"Don't worry about it." Shanika body shuddered as she melted in my arms.

"Go back to that bitch." She spat.

"Watchu' mean? I'm with my bitch," I mumbled, kissing her lips.

"Tell that hoe that you're done with her and if I ever catch you with her again, I'mma whoop some sense into her thick headed ass," Shanika spoke loud enough for Eliza to hear.

Turning to face Eliza, I smirked.

"You heard what my baby mama said."

"Nigga fuck you and her! I'm happy I got rid of that baby!" Eliza yelled out thinking that was going to earn her the open hand.

Shanika tried to jump at her, but I held her back.

"Just chill and let me explain," I said before filling her in on the baby Eliza aborted.

"If I ever catch you with scandalous bitch again, I'mma fuck you up then I'mma fuck her up, do you hear me?!" Shanika placed a hand on her hip while she snake her neck, laying down the fucking law.

I couldn't front that shit was lowkey sexy as fuck. Then she had a nerve to pull up on a nigga dressed in all black, my dick was hard.

Pregnancy looked good on Shanika. The way her skin glowed made her even more beautiful, I didn't even think that shit was possible. Lil man was already looking out for his mama the way he had Shanika hips spreading and ass thickening. Shanika only complaint was her nose doubling in size, but even her fat ass nose was sexy to me. The essence of a woman carrying your baby was a beautiful thing. Duke wasn't here yet and my mind was already on baby number two.

"I hear you." I nodded. "Now let me take you to the hospital so I can check on my son."

"He's fine."

"Nah, you were just doing the most. I need to make sure my lil nigga good for myself.'

"I'll meet you there," Shanika slickly said, I wasn't falling for that shit though.

"I'll have Ti Zoe drop your car off at the crib. Let's go." Pecking Shanika's lips a final time, I pulled her into my arms before wrapping an arm around her neck.

Chucking up the duces at Eliza, I walked Shanika to my car so I could take her to the hospital. Once I made sure my lil man was good, I fed Shanika all the shit I normally wouldn't let her eat before behind her over the balcony and feeding her some dick.

*****

Glancing over at Shanika in awe, I watched as she sat with her pretty white chubby toes against my windshield while she sat in the passenger seat with a laptop in her lap. While I was making runs, Shanika was creating plays. I respected her hustle but couldn't help but to think about the chances she was taking.

"Turn right there?" Shanika instructed over Future, *Fuck Up Some Commas*. The song matched the mood since we both was on the grind, fucking up some commas.

"Here?" I pointed to the old house that was boarded up.

"Uh huh," Shanika nodded.

Pulling up to the house, I paralleled parked. Shanika hoped out of the car with a yellow envelope filled with duplicate credits card and IDs in her hand before tucking it behind some bushes. Shanika made sure the envelope was discreetly hidden before walking back to the car and getting in.

Pulling out her burner phone, Shanika texted her customer letting them know the order was fulfilled and where to pick the package up from.

"Now we can go eat." Shanika beamed, shutting the untraceable laptop closed then tucking it under the back seat.

"When are you going to be done with this shit?" I asked. She was still camming and pregnant and although I respected her dedication to the grind, the well-being of my baby mattered more.

"I'm done for the day." She announced.

"I mean done for good." I looked over at her.

"I'll stop scamming when you stop selling drugs." Shanika pursed her lips, crossing her arm over her chest.

"Nah, that ain't happening. I'm the man I should be the only one taking penitentiary chances."

"What the fuck am I supposed to do for money?" she shrieked.

"Don't insult my intelligence, Shanika. I ain't out here pushing twice the amount of weight I'd normally push for fun. I'm out here securing our baby's future.'

"That's good and all for the baby, but I need money for myself. I need to make sure I'm good." Shanika pounded on her chest.

"Aye chill before you hurt my baby," I warned. I didn't want to turn a simple conversation into a shouting match.

"All I'm saying is, I'm doing what I'm doing to make sure my future is secured."

"Then what?"

"I'll figure it out when I cross that bridge."

"Do you even hear yourself?" I huffed. "You sounding like one of these corner boys on the block, hustling without a plan.

"Since you got it, all figured out, what do you suggest I do?"

"Find something you're good at or interested in and use it to flip yo money. We got a baby coming in a few months. I can't have us both on the frontlines risking it all. I'll sleep better knowing that you're not out here with a target on your back."

"Nobody knows I'm Tiffany." She stressed.

"That's not the point, ma. Our son needs you. I'm not asking you to be a stay at home mom. Shit, you can if you want to be. I'm just saying find a legal way to make your money."

"I've always wanted to open an accounting firm."

"I can dig it," I nodded my head in approval. "You have my full support to go back to school."

"I already have my accounting degree, I got it when I was locked up," Shanika nonchalantly revealed as if her having a degree wasn't a big deal.

"Are you for real?" I briefly glanced over at her. "Why you never said nothing?"

"I didn't think it was a big deal," she shrugged.

"That's a big fucking deal, shorty! I'm happy as fuck for you right now, no lie," I said, thinking of ways to celebrate her accomplishment.

"Nobody knows I got my degree. I don't know why I never said anything about it, I guess I didn't think it mattered since I got it behind bars."

"It don't give a fuck if you got your degree under the sea, it matters!' I assured her with a huge smile. I was proud of her, for real.

"Why haven't you put your degree to use?"

"When I first got out, my initial plan was to hustle up enough money to help Lisa open her boutique then my firm, but I guess I got addicted to the fast money. It's something about playing with number to make money that gives me a rush. That's probably why I got an accountant degree. This life... this life got a hold on me and no matter how hard I try to let it go, I feel like I can't." Shanika explained.

It was as if she was preaching to the choir because I knew the feeling all too well.

"Alright how about this, keep running it up until the baby is born. The moment Duke is here you gotta stop." I offered, willing to compromise.

"Deal." Shanika held her hand out for me to shake.

"Nah thing I'm gon' be shaking is this dick right before I put it in you," I smirked.

"You so nasty!" she giggled, shaking her head.

"Who told you to have pussy so fucking good?" I chuckled, heading to the spot of my final drop.

Once I dropped this load off, I planned on taking the next two weeks off to pamper my baby mama. I had been secretly texting Carlene planning a quick trip. Duke arrival was going to change our lives, so this was my way of us enjoying the calm before the storm.

Chapter Ten
Damos "Haiti" Pierre

Rocking my baby boy in my arms, my chest swelled with proud. Eight weeks ago, Shanika endured fifteen hours of labor that resulted in the birth of my first-born son, Duke Pierre. My heart was full. I didn't think it was possible to love a little human as much as I loved him, but here this lil nigga was making me all emotional and shit.

"My nigga," I smiled down at him before walking over to the bathroom and standing in the doorway.

I watched as Shanika's aunt gave her a final Bain, which was a traditional Haitian after birth bath that consisted of many different herbs and leaves. As she sat on the metal bucket covered with a blanket, my dick jumped at the thought of finally getting some pussy. After waiting six long weeks for her to get cleared by her doctor and another two weeks for her to complete her remedy bath, tonight was finally the night.

"Why you looking at me like I'm a piece of meat?" Shanika asked, as she stood from the bucket of water.

"Wait until tonight," I mouthed out of respect for her aunt.

Shanika's aunt was in her own world humming a Haitian tune as she bonded Shanika's belly with a long, thick cloth. Today was her last day being wrapped in that too. The bloating in Shanika's belly had significantly gone down thanks to our cultural postpartum care. I was tripping though, I loved the extra thickness Duke left Shanika with.

Once Shanika's was clothed from head to toe, her aunt led her to the bed before handing her a cup of ginger tea. In the Haitian culture it was tradition for the mother to occupy the caregiver role. Shanika's aunt had filled that role beautifully. The moment Shanika went into labor she'd been staying here with us, bathing Shanika, giving her tea, fixing her meals, and helping her breast feed.

"Li lè pou mwen ale. Rele m si w bezwen. *Its time for me to leave now. Call me if you ned me."* Shanika's aunt said gathering her things, preparing to leave. The eight weeks she'd been here with us had been a blessing.

Since Duke was drinking breast milk from the breast and a bottle, Shanika's aunt came in clutch when it came to the nighttime feedings. From the daily homecooked meals and rest, she had us spoiled for real.

"Mèsi, mommy. *Thank you, mommy."* Shanika hugged then kissed her aunt.

"Mèsi anpil. *Thank you, a lot."* I said, hugging her too.
"Pa gen pwoblèm pitit gason m. Mwen gen asa manje prepare pou twa jou. Enjoy. *No problem, son. I have enough food prepared for three days. Enjoy."* She replied.

"Alright, girl I'mma hit you up to later," Lisa hugged Shanika then looked down at the baby.

"It should be illegally to look this damn cute," Lisa cooed before saying her final *goodbyes* then following her mother out of the door.

Locking the door behind them, I placed Duke in his crib that was attached to Shanika's side of the bed before laying down next to her.

Duke had an entire Giraffe themed nursey that he barley slept in. Buying one of those bedside bassinets made better since for nighttime feeding and care.

"Can I get some pussy now?" I pressed, sloppily kissing her.

"Horny ass! I got you with some pussy tonight, I promise. I been feigning for the dick too, daddy," she purred making my dick thump.

"Suck for me while he sleep," I pleaded, tugging at hair.

Shanika's ginger colored hair had grown a little past her neck. Lisa cut and styled Shanika's hair into what she referred to as a blunt bob and I couldn't lie, I was fucking with that hair style.

"Anything for you daddy." Shanika licked her lips before pulling my dick out then swallowing it whole.
*****

WHAP!

I swift smack to the face pulled me out of the trance I was in. I was laying on the swinging canopy bed by the pool smoking a blunt with Shanika hit me. Looking up, I spotted Shanika standing over me rocking a menacing scowl, holding a box of condoms in her hand.

Fuck!

"What the fuck are these?" she angrily asked, cocking her head to the side while she stared at me with menacing eyes.

"Condoms. Why wassup?" I coolly spoke.

"I know what the fuck these are, why do you have them?"

"We about to start fucking soon and I just wanted to be prepared in case you wanted me to strap up," I said the first thing that came to my mind.

"So, I'm guessing there's a condom missing from the box because you wanted to test them out before using them on me, huh?"

"Nah," I gulped shaking my head. "I been had those," I swiftly mumbled.

"You bought these condoms two weeks!" she tossed the receipt in my face.

Glancing down at the date, my mind traveled back to the night I almost fucked another bitch. Earlier that day we had come home from Shanika's six week appointment. I thought I was going to get some pussy until I learned she had two more weeks of *healing*. That night, after wrapping up business with the crew, we fell through at a strip club. A couple of blunts and a half bottle of Remy later, I was driving to the nearest store while the shorty I picked up from the club sucked my dick.

Once I had the condom in place, I was getting ready to smash shorty until I was consumed by guilt. Thoughts of my Shanika at home with my baby plagued my mind. When I realized I glanced at the time and noticed it was close to Duke's feeding time, I told shorty it was a wrap. I gave her a couple of dollars for her troubles, dropped her off back to the club then went home to tend to my son.

"So, you want me to believe that you almost fucked a bitch?" she frowned.

"I mean, that's what happened." I truthfully replied.

"I pushed your baby out of my fucking pussy and you replay me by fucking another bitch?"

"Man, I ain't fuck that girl she sucked my dick!"

"Same fucking difference, Damos!" she shouted in my face.

"I'm not about to sit around here and go for a nigga cheating on me, nah! I'm done!"

"Done with what exactly?" I questioned, trying to understand why she was so mad.

"This," she pointed from me to her. "Us. We're over!"

"It ain't like we're in a committed relationship or no shit like that, so technically I ain't do nothing wrong." I breathed out, instantly regretting my choice of words the moment they fell from my lips.

"We're not in a relationship?" she chuckled, the huffed.

"I ain't even mean it like that," I deeply exhaled, feeling as If I was doing more damage to the situation than I was good.

I was trying to avoid an unnecessary argument, but I could feel some bullshit brewing.

"You get me pregnant, force me to live in this fucking house with you, we have this baby together. So, you tell me. What the fuck are we doing?!" she shouted so loud that I was sure Duke heard her

"We're co-parenting."

"I don't live in this fucking house with you in order for us to co-parent!"

"Well, I'm not trying to live in a house without my son! You jumping down my back like I'm wrong. I respected your mind since the day I found out you. I've been there for you and Duke every step of the way. I handle my responsibilities like a man. I did everything I promised, Shanika. I never promised you a relationship and you never brought up us being in one," I truthfully said.

Shanika stressed that she wanted me to be there for the baby, but she never mentioned us being in a relationship.

"We got a lot of shit to figure out then because I'm not staying where I'm not wanted." Shanika, feet looked like baby feet in my sandals as she angrily tapped them against the floor.

Pinching the bridge of my nose, I sighed.

"I didn't say you was wanted here."

"Nah, you just made it clear that we're not together."

"You never made it clear that you wanted us to be together!" I shouted.

"You know what, fuck you and fuck this!" she yelled, storming off, almost tripping off her feet because my shoes were way too big for her.

Dropping my head, I shook it then chuckled.

"This girl is going to be the reason I'm taking Lisinopril," I mumbled to myself, re-lighting my blunt then taking a few desperate pulls. When I was done smoking, I went to the bar and took a shot of Hennessy to ease my mind before venturing up the stairs to deal with Shanika.

"This nigga got me fucked up if he thinks I'm about to sit here and let him play me like a fiddle. I'm not a fucking clown so I'm not about to participate in his circus. Fuck him!" Shanika incoherently ranted as she stuffed her clothes into suitcases.

"You working yourself up for nothing," I said, glancing at my son who was peacefully sleeping in his crib.

"Shut the fuck up talking to me!" she harshly whispered. No matter how mad Shanika got, she knew not to disturb Duke's sleep. I love my lil nigga, but jit had some lungs on him.

"You not leaving this house with my son!"

"I pushed Duke out of my pussy, that's my son. I can take him wherever the fuck I please. If you got a problem, take me to court!" she lashed out.

Duke stirred in his sleep. Gently patting his round belly, I slowly rocked him until he was sleeping peacefully again.

Stepping into Shanika's personal space, I gripped her plump ass. The oversized clothes she was forced to wear after birth were now replaced with a satin cami top and shorts pajamas set, underneath the matching satin robe. Shanika's hair was wrapped in a scarf, her face was fresh, and she smelt sweet.

"Get the fuck off of me," Shanika fought me off, but I was stronger.

"Why you tryna take my baby and leave me?" I asked, licking her earlobe.

"We're not together, remember?" she huffed.

"Stop playing with me, Nika," I cornered her, dipping my head to peck her lips.

She was resistant at first, but when I started toying with her clit, she gave in.

"Mmm," she moaned against my lips, her body shaking at my touch.

"This pussy so fucking wet." I pulled my fingers from his pussy showing her how drenched she had them.

"I missed this pussy." Smearing Shanika's pussy juices against her lips, I licked it off.

"Can I have some pussy?" I begged, pulling of her nipples out then licking all over them.

I didn't give a fuck if she was breastfeeding, I was willing to get a little milk in my mouth if it meant making Shanika feel good. Shit, from what I heard breastmilk was good for practically everything.

"No," she whimpered as her body melted in my arms.

"Please?" I ran my finger over her wet slit before twirling her clit as a stress relief ball and firmly yet gently rolling it between my fingers.

"Oh shit!" she panted, opening her legs wider so I can slip two fingers in her.

Removing her shorts, I carried her to the hallway. Resting her against the wall, I held her up then slid her down my dick.

"FUCK!" we both cried out.

The reconnection after two months felt good. The feeling of Shanika's gushy pussy sucking my dick in then pushing It out had my toes gripping the carpet for mercy. I was so deep in it, that I couldn't stop if I wanted to. Three minutes later I was feeling her up.

"Damn," I groaned, sucking on her neck while I regained my composure.

Back peddling into the guest bedroom with my tongue down Shanika's mouth, I laid her body on the bed before kissing my way down south.

"Oh daddddddddyyyyy," Shanika purred, locking her legs around my head.

I was drowning in her wetness, but I refused to let up. Shit, if a nigga was going to die, I wouldn't mine it being like this

*****

Whaaaaa! Whaaaaa! Whaaaaa!

Duke's loud cries pulled me out of the sexually induced coma I was in, forcing me to my feet. Looking over to Shanika's side of the bed, she was gone. My dick was saturated with Shanika's dried up juices as it swung with every step I took.

"Shanika! I called out entering the bathroom.

Quickly washing my dick in the sink, I washed my hands then got dressed in a pair of grey sweats.

"Shanika!" I yelled, picking up Duke and cradling him in my arms.

Descending the stairs, I stopped in the kitchen to warm up one of Duke's breastmilk bottle before feeding it to him.

"Where your mama at?" I asked Duke, continuing my search for Shanika.

After searching every square inch of the home, I realized Shanika wasn't home.

"Duke ya mama tripping," I sighed plopping down into the rocking chair.

Clutching Duke in a football hold I used my chest to hold the bottle in his mouth while I scrolling through my phone with my free hand.

"Aye man, call me back when you get this message." I finally left a voicemail after my tenth call went unanswered.

Scrolling down my contacts, I called Lisa and her mom. They both claimed they didn't know where Shanika was, nor did they sound alarmed that she was missing.

"How the fuck you gon' lave Duke here with no food? What the fuck am I supposed to feed him? Bring yo ass home, man! Aye Shanika, if I have to come looking for you it won't be nothing nice." I barked into the phone before hanging up.

Shanika was big on pumping, so Duke had his own milk. I even bough him his personal deep freezer so Shanika could properly store his milk. I didn't give a fuck about none of that shit though, Shanika needed to bring her ass home.

Startled by the ringing of the phone, I answered it without checking the caller ID thinking Shanika was finally returning my calls.

"Yo, Haiti I gotta holla at you about some shit!" Stone, a member of DCHB said.

"I ain't handling business today, call that nigga Ti Zoe!"

"It ain't business."

"Then what the fuck you want?" I snapped, I already had my own personal shit going own, I wasn't trying to deal with no one else's bullshit.

"Check me out," he paused then sighed. "My lil brother was on one of those dating sites. He swiping and shit and fucks around and swipe on Shanika."

My heart stopped.

"The fuck you mean he swiped on Shanika?!" I belted out, causing Duke to jump then cry.

"My bad lil man," I cooed, placing him over my shoulder so that I could burp him.

"Listen, my brother ain't from the streets, he a football player at Ohio State. He didn't know Shanika was your girl until I told him.

"So, what the fuck happened?"

"He said they met up and kicked it," Stone replied.

I started seeing red.

"What the fuck you mean, *they kicked it*?" I roared.

"That's all I know my boy. He asked me to pick him up from this bar, and that's when I spotted him and Shanika hugging and shit. I told my brother what was up with shorty, and he instantly block her. I'm telling you this shit out of respect but coming for my brother is a no go," Stone explained.

"Good looking out, man." I mumbled ending our call.

The thought of another nigga fucking Shanika right after me left me sick to my stomach. I wanted to fuck Stone's brother up, but the lil nigga didn't know who Shanika was therefore, he wasn't stepping on my toes. My beef was with Shanika not him.

Changing Duke's diaper, I changed his clothes then rocked him back to sleep. Once he was down, I called my sister to babysit for me. I headed to the closet to get dressed.

"What the fuck is this?" I mumbled stumbling over a MCM duffle bag.

I didn't remember purchasing this bag or seeing Shanika with it for that matter. Alarmed, I shuffled through the bag, then frowned. Tucked discreetly in blank folders were paperwork for unemployment with names of different people from different states on them. Instantly the wheels in my head started turning.

"Nah, she wouldn't lie to me like that," I shook my head in disbelief as I pulled out bank ATM slips with different amount of money on them. The balances on each slip ranging from five thousand to thirty thousand dollars.

Shanika and I agreed that when Duke entered this world, she would stop scamming. When we came home from our two-day hospital stay, I watched as she got rid of everything associated to her hustle, or so I thought. To make good on my word, I hired a realtor to help Shanika find the perfect location for her accounting firm, I even told her I was going to purchase the building. Shanika excuse was that she wanted to bind for Duke first, but now I see that shit was a lie.

"Shorty knee deep in the game," I mumbled, retrieving the burner phone that was tucked in one of the pockets, along with debit cards that matched the names on the unemployment documents.

"Where's my cute little stinka butt?" Carlene asked, walking into the room followed by Dina.

Quickly stuffing everything in the bag, I threw on the first thing I saw then grabbed the bag, tossing it over my shoulder.

"Y'all gotta learn how to knock." I smiled at my sisters, pulling them both in for a hug.

"Oh hush, you wouldn't have given us the keypad code if you didn't want us just barging in," Carlene waved me off.

While Dina picked the baby up.

"He's sleeping." I sighed.

"So what? The job of an auntie is to spoil them rotten then give them back to their parents." Dina spoke, while Carlene looked over her shoulders at the baby.

Seeing my sister interact with Duke made my heart smile. The thing Duke was missing in his life was his paternal grandparents. My sister told them about Duke being born, but they never bothered to reach out. I was hurt, but then I realized I wasn't going to force anyone to be a part of my son's life.

"If he run through the milk in the refrigerator, he has more in the deep freezer. Just thaw it out then—"

"I work in the pediatric unit, I know how to care for babies," Dina cut me off.

"Well alright then, nurse. I shouldn't be gone long. Call me if you need me." Kissing Duke on the forehead, I rushed out the house before they could question me about Shanika's whereabouts. Especially Dina.

Dina was still salty over Eliza deciding to become a travel nurse. My last encounter with Eliza placed a wedge between the two best friends and Dina blamed me for that. She blamed Shanika too. Dina didn't dislike Shanika, but she wasn't trying to become friends with her either.

Checking the cameras on the app I had installed on my phone, I hopped in my ride then pulled off.

Chapter Eleven
Shanika St. Mark

"Big ole freak. Big booty, big ole treat I'mma make him wait for the pussy, hit it 'til he big ole skeet," I rapped the lyrics to *Big Ole Freak,* by Megan Thee Stallion with my whole chest as I stuck my key into my door, unlocking it.

Stepping into my apartment, I quickly closed the door then locked it behind me. Dropping my keys, purse and phone on the ground, my heels tapped against the tile as I quickly ran to the bathroom to relieve my bladder. Plopping down on the toilet, I kicked my heels off then sighed. The turn up was real. After linking up with this college football player, Benny, and getting my pussy ate as if it was that nigga's last mean, I went bar hopping with my cousin, Lisa. It's been a minute since I been outside on some bald-headed hoe shit and tonight. Well, let's just say tonight was one for the books.

Standing from the toilet I wiped myself, washed my hands, then made my way to the kitchen to enjoy my Waffle House.

"You done being a hoe?" A deep shrilling voice said, startling me.

Looking over at the island, Haiti was seated on one of my bar stools eating my Waffle House meal. I didn't see him when I came it, I didn't even know how he got in for that matter. I haven't stayed in this apartment since I moved in with Haiti, but I made sure to pay the rent every month, I even renewed the lease. Haiti was against it, to soothe his ego I told him I got rid of the place amongst other things, but in reality, I would never put that much trust in a nigga that wasn't my husband.

"How did you get in here?" I asked, glancing down at my empty container of food.

"Why did you eat all of my fucking food?!" I angrily fumed. I had been drinking like a fish and smoking like a chimney. Although I wasn't passed the legal limit, I was fucked up and needed something nice and greasy on my stomach.

"That shit was fye too," he smirked, before gulping down my drink then wiping his mouth with a napkin.

"Where the fuck you been?" he stood inching towards.

"Minding my fucking business. Where is my son?"

"Oh now you worried about my son. You wasn't worried about him when you was out there thotting and bopping."

"I left my son in the care of his father, with more than enough breastmilk to last him for a month. I don't see nothing wrong with that."

"You don't see nothing wrong with abandoning your son so you can fuck niggas?" he winced at the thought of another nigga between my legs.

That shit was funny to me. Niggas were funny in general. Haiti had just told me that we wasn't in a committed relationship now he was over here trying to keep tabs on my pussy.

"I'm not about to argue with you, Haiti," I waved him off, making. Beeline to the kitchen. I needed to find something to soak up this liquor, but since I barley lived here there was barley anything to eat.

"You not about to argue with me, huh?" Haiti chuckled. "You full of fucking surprises, I fucked around and put a baby in a lying hoe!"

He lunged my MCM duffle bag at my feet. I gulped. I was in a rush trying to sneak out of the house while Haiti and Duke slept that I forgot to take the duffle bag with me.

"I thought you was done scamming?" he probed.

Leaning against the counter, I nibbled on the corner of my lip.

"You ain't got shit to say?" Haiti angrily pressed.

"What the fuck you want me to say, Haiti?"

"Tell me why yo ass being so sneaky! You still scamming, you kept this apartment after you told me you got rid of it, now you're on hook up sites meeting up with random niggas for sex! What the fuck is wrong with you?"

"Ain't shit wrong with me," I hunched my shoulders. "What the fuck is wrong with you? Last time I checked I was single and free to do whatever the fuck I please. What I do don't concern you!"

"It does when it affects my son!"

"Nigga, please!" I waved him off. "You a pot calling the kettle black ass nigga. You taking the same chances I am, yet you wanna breathed down my fucking neck, nigga fuck you!" I called out, flaring my arms from side to side.

"You're a fucking mother!" he raged, peering at me with furry in his eyes.

"And you're a fucking father!" I shot back.

"I'm a man my job is to take care of home and make sure the two of you straight, I did that!"

"And I'm a woman that's going to always make sure she have her own. I'm not putting my life in the hands of a nigga that I'm not even in a committed relationship. Nah. I ain't even about to play myself like that!"

"You ain't have to depend on me financially, we had a fucking agreement! You had a plan! I made sure you had your LLC, your EIN number, I gotchu the realtor and the start up money. You could've been focusing on your accounting firm, yet you tryna puff yo chest out like you a nigga or some shit with a point to prove."

Tucking my bottom lip in my mouth, I remained silent.

Haiti did everything he could to help me go legit, but I wasn't ready. I loved my son and understood the risk I was taking, but the thrill of scamming had me in a chokehold. Walking away was easier said than done.

"Did you fuck that nigga?" Haiti asked, pulling me from my thoughts.

"Nah," I shook my head.

Stepping in my personal space, Haiti twisted my head to the side, running his thumb against the passion mark that was on my neck.

"DID YOU FUCK THAT NIGGA?!" he asked me again, this time he was gripping my chin.

"Nope, he just ate my pussy." I looked in his eyes then smirked.

"You think this shit is funny, huh?"

"Yeah, I think YOU'RE funny. You were just hollering about you being a single man, now you wanna give me static because I'm out here living my best life."

"You a nasty hoe! You left my house with my nut still in you to fuck another nigga, you foul as fuck," Haiti frowned, looking down at me in disgust.

"I took a shower, first."

BOOM!

Haiti punched a big hole in the wall above my head.

"You paying for that shit," I said stepping away for him, making my way to my phone that was on the counter next to where Haiti was sitting. I was sure he went through my phone, and he was feeling sick right now, but that didn't have shit to do with me.

I spent four years behind bars because I fucked around and lost myself behind a nigga, I wasn't doing that shit again.

Blood from Haiti's knuckles trickled all over my white tile as he made his way to the sink to apply pressure on his wound with one of my dish towels.

Sending Lisa a quick SOS texted, I busied myself with scrolling through my phone.

"Don't even bother deleting shit, I already saw how your hoe ass get down."

"I guess," I mumbled then shrugged.

I was done arguing with Haiti, that back and forth shit was for the birds. He showed me his hand now he wanna cry and shit because I knew how to play the game too. Fuck him. As soon as Lisa pulled up, I was picking up my son then heading to my aunt's house for a couple of days. Haiti was stupid, but he knew better than to start some shit at an older Haitian's house.

"Hello?" I answered my ringing phone.

Wassup mama?" Zed, dude I met at the bar earlier responded in a tone that made my pussy thump.

Fine ass Zed.

The minute I started up conversation with the six feet, milk chocolate, athletic built Greek God, he was persistent. He joined me and Lisa and we traveled bar to bar getting fucked up then shaking our asses on the tabletops. At the end of our night, he ate my pussy and ass in the back seat of his car until I begged him to stop.

In one night, I had two different niggas licking on my twat like a lollipop. Call me what you want, but I was making up for lost time. I had four years stripped from me, then another fucking around with Haiti, now it was time for me to live my best hoe life.

"Shit, you tell me," I flirted, doing the most since Haiti was huffing and puffing while watching me like a hawk.

The head was magnificent, but I didn't see myself fucking with Zed. Zed was the type of nigga that wouldn't know how to be a sneaky link. He gave off the vibe that he was a fall in love type of nigga, the type of ma'fucka that'll fuck around and stalk me after he sampled my pussy. I was lowkey kicking myself for not blocking his ass, but then again, it ended up working out in my favor since Haiti was all in my mouth trying to catch some tea.

I was about to send his ass home, crying in his fucking Lamborghini truck.

"You want me to fall through so we can finish what we started?" Zed asked in a low, sultry tone.

Glancing over at Haiti, I smiled. He was pissed and I was playing with fire.

"I'm about to send you my location now," I lied.

"Make sure you bring the—"

WHAP!

Haiti smacked the phone out of my hand.

"Are you for real right now?" he growled picking up the phone sop he could talk.

"My man, if you know what's good for you, you'll lose this fucking number!" he grunted before ending the call.

Dropping my phone on the floor, he stomped it with his big ass feet, shattering it into pieces.

"You gon' replace my fucking phone!" I yelled in his face.

Gripping me by the neck, Haiti backed me into a wall.

"You think this shit a fucking game?" he grilled me.

"I don't think shit! We not together so get the fuck out of my house so I can do me. When I'm done we can discuss how we'll handle Duke, until then move around before my new nigga come through," I said, taunting his ass with a devious smile.

BOOM! BOOM!

He punched two more holes in my wall.

"Keep playing with me!" he yelled out as he began fucking up everything that was in my house.

BOOM!

My TV was on the floor shattered.

BOOM!

My expensive decorated vases.

BOOM!

He kicked a fucking hold in the wall like a fucking lunatic.

"You going to fuck around and get me put out!" I shrieked, looking around at all the damages in horror.

"I don't give a fuck, bitch!" he spat, pushing me out the way so he could vandalize my dining room set.

"I paid for all this shit, remember?" he mumbled as he traveled room to room fucking everything up.

"Oh, you got me fucked!" I lost it when he started destroying my *work* equipment.

Running up on him, I threw a wild punch that caught him in the jaw.

Haiti was pissed, but I was furious.

I didn't give a fuck about all the material shit, but this nigga was fucking with my money and that was no go.

WHAP! WHAP!

I swung my fists catching him two more times in the jaw, this time drawing blood. On some karate shit, I jumped up as high as I could then kicked his ass in the chest.

"You fucking crazy!" Haiti growled, pulling me by the wig Lisa just installed, snatching it off my head.

Haiti gritted his teeth so restrain himself from hitting me back, but when I popped him in the nose he lost his cool.

"Chill the fuck out!" he barked, grabbing me by my shoulders then shaking.

My head violently rocked back and forth while Haiti shook as if I was a rag doll. Throwing me against the wall, he wrapped a hand around my neck then tightened his grasp.

"Why you acting like I won't snap ya fucking neck and leave yo ass right here?!" he grunted, slowly cutting my air supply off.

Deeply exhaling Haiti tossed me on the floor.

"I'mma go before I fuck around and really put hands on yo ass! You can have this shit, all of it. Keep scamming, be a hoe, do whatever the fuck you want to do. You wanna be so fucking free, well you're free. I'm done witchu'! Don't worry about my son, he done witcho ass too!"

My chest caved at Haiti's admission of being done with me, but the mention of him trying to take my son away from me sit me into blinded rage. Hopping off the floor as if it was on fire, I jumped on Haiti's back then started punching him in the head. Haiti spun around trying to shake me off of him, but my hold on him was tight. Sinking my teeth in his neck, I drew blood.

"Ahhh! FUCK!" He cried out in pain.

Haiti back into a wall slamming me against it.

"Ouch!" I cried out, letting his neck go I fell to the ground.

"Stupid ass," he mumbled trying to get away, but my feelings were hurt and I wasn't letting him walk away from me so easily.

Running back up on Haiti, I hit him with a swift uppercut to the jaw before we started tussling. Pictures were falling off the walls, as we traveled wall to wall tearing the house up.

"SHANIKA!" Lisa called out, rushing over to us.

"Get the fuck off of her!" she yelled out, struggling to pull Haiti off on me.

He had my ass pinned down to the ground and I couldn't move.

"Tell ya cousin to chill the fuck out man! I wasn't even tryna do all this with her," Haiti signed, getting off of me.

"I will fuck yo stupid ass up," I huffed, trying to go after his ass again but Lisa held me back.

"Lisa let me go!" I barked at her.

"No, Shanika! You fucked that nigga up enough. Let him go." Lisa held on tightly to me.

My chest rapidly rose then fell as I looked over at Haiti through angry slits. If looks could kill that nigga would be dead. Haiti's face was covered in blood, cuts and bruises. Compared to me, he looked more like the battered victim than I did. If the police was to show up right now, I was sure I'd be the one to go to jail on a domestic violence charge.

"He's trying to take my baby from me," I sobbed. Duke was everything to me, the thought of not being in his life was unbearable.

"Yup, come get him back in blood!" Haiti spat before rushing out of the house.

"We gotta go get my baby! That nigga can't take my baby!" I ranted, with tears falling from my eyes.

"Just relax. You know Duke is in good hands with his daddy. Let's just go to the house and chill and we'll pick him up in the morning once everything dies down." Lisa gave me an assuring smile.

Pausing, she did a full three- sixty assessing the damages that was done.

"You ain't getting your deposit back," she said. We both laughed.

Chapter Twelve
Damos "Haiti" Pierre

"Yo, you straight?" Ti Zoe asked me, pulling me out of my thoughts.

"Yeah, nigga. I'm good," I replied. Clearing my throat, I adjusted myself in my seat uninterested in the *pick me* strippers that were practically throwing their pussy in my face.

"Then throw some fucking money, smack some ass, do something! Shit, all these bad ass bitches in this section and you wanna sulk and shit!" Ti Zoe tossed a shot back before popping the band of a stack of bill then making it rain.

Physically I was at the strip club throwing it up for my dawg, Ti Zoe's birthday but mentally I was elsewhere. I was missing my family. It's been three months I last laid eyes on Shanika and a nigga was sick. I had unlimited access to my son, but Lisa played mediator. She was the middleman that transported Duke back and forth between homes. I hated our currently arrangement, but I had nobody to blame but myself.

I didn't know nothing about postpartum depression until Dina sat me down and explained it to me in detail. Sure, I was there for my son and Shanika catering to their every need, but I was selfish. I gave Shanika full access to me, my time, my space under the pretenses that we were building then threw in her face that we weren't in a committed relationship. I fucked up.

Finishing off my blunt, I took a shot then stood up.

"I'm out y'all boys," I shouted over the music.

"Watchu' mean you out," Ti Zoe stood, then stumbled. He was fucked up, but I didn't expect anything less from the birthday boy. That nigga was a real party animal.

"I'm about to go handle some shit," I said turning to face Bozo. "Aye make sure this nigga gets home safely, if he fucking a bitch make sure yo ass standing guard by the door,' I ordered to one of our henchmen.

Ti Zoe was rolling real hard and I didn't need no nigga or bitch setting him up.

"I gotchu'." Bozo nodded.

"You about to run home, ol crying, Keith Sweat ass nigga!" Ti Zoe chuckled.

"Fuck you, nigga!" I laughed before making my way out of the section.

On my way to my car, I was bombarded by a plethora of bitches. Each of them wanting to be the one I ended my night with, but I curved them all strongarming the few that were bold enough to follow me to my car. Hopping in my ride, I pulled off, heading to a destination I only visited on birthdays and holidays.

"Stacy, baby wassup?" I greeted the tombstone, before plopping down on the wet grass.

"I know you wondering why I'm here right now, but I needed to talk," I sighed, glancing around the dark gravesite.

"I met this girl, had a baby, fell in love and got scared. I'm so fucking scared of loving another woman and have her leave me the way you did. I'm fucked up, ma!" I sadly mumbled.

"When you died, my ability to love another female died with you. Shanika ass changed that though. Shorty was just supposed to be an easy lay, but I fucked around and got soul tied now a nigga can't eat, sleep or hustle in peace because I'm all heartbroken and shit." I paused then chuckle.

"I know yo ass up there having a field day hearing that your man out here going out sad behind a broad, but in my defense, she's worth it. I love her, Stacy. I love Shanika and I need to you go so I can love her properly." Picking at the grass that was by my feet, I inhaled then deeply exhaled.

"I will always love you Stacy and nothing will ever change that, but I gotta let you go so I can move on." I licked my lips then turned to face the tombstone.

"Stacy baby, I'm moving on and allowing myself to fall in love again. Thank you for being my first love, for being the true embodiment of love is. I found that again on Shanika and I'm willing to do anything not to lose it. I can't lose her, ma. I'll go crazy if I lose her." I dropped my head, palming my low fade.

"I know a nigga not making any sense right now, but I hope you can understand where I'm coming from."

In silence, I sat there allowing my thoughts to run wildly in my head. Instantly a feeling of peace washed over me. It was as if Stacy was telling me, it was ok to move on and love without limits.

"I hear you baby and I love you too." I kissed the tombstone then stood. I felt like a heavy weight was lifted off my shoulders as I walked back to my car.

I was ready to get my girl back, but first I had one more stop to me.

*****

"Are you ready?" Carlene asked the moment she opened the front door.

"I have no choice but to be," I replied, crossing the threshold of my parents' home for the first time.

It was crazy this was my first time seeing the home fully furniture since I was the one that purchased it, but I wasn't tripping on that. Today, I needed to make amends with my parents. I was making peace with everything in my life holding me back. I had to do this if I ever wanted to have a healthy relationship with Shanika and our son.

"Kisa wap fè la? *What are you doing here?*" my father grunted the moment he spotted me. The anger in his voice was evident as he stood there looking at me with disgust in his eyes. I

By his side was my mother. She looked at me with remorse as she stood their supporting her husband. That was the shit I hate about growing up in a Haitian household. Even if your mother was willing to love you through your mistakes, the moment your father decided to disown you they had no choice but to agree.

"Mwen bezwen pale ak ou. *I need to talk to you,*" I said.

"Mwen pa gen anyen poum di ou. *I don't have anything to say to you.*" My father snapped, he was about to walk away but my mother stopped him

"Koute sa mwen gen pou di. *Listen to what I have to say,*" I pleaded, looking from him to my mother.

My father nodded as if to tell me to speak. Licking my lips, I cleared my throat before explaining to my father why I took the chances I did.

"Mwen pa janm sispan renmen ou. Mwen fache avek lavi ou chawzi. *I never stopped loving you. I'm angry with the way you decided to live your life.*" My father revealed. Hearing him say he never stopped loving me brought me a sense of peace.

"Mwen fé sa mwen fè pou nou! *I did what I do for us!*" I explained.

"Mwen pa t 'mande ou! *I didn't ask you!*" He countered.

After going back and forth with my dad about his role as the man of the house and how it was his responsibility to take care of us, not mine. We decided to just agree to disagree. Seeing the tears fall from my mother's eyes broke my heart. Taking slow strides towards her, I wrapped my hands around her small, short frame. We rocked side to side while she sobbed thanking God for bringing her only son back into her life.

My father patted me on the back, then pulled me in his arms.

"I love you my son," he spoke with a thick accent.

"I love you too, dad" I sniffled, trying my best to blink back my tears.

Real niggas didn't cry, but this moment was very emotional for me. To have my parents admit that they never stopped loving me, felt good. Having them welcome me back into the family with open arms despite my hood ties, was all I ever wanted.

"Where is de baby?" my mother asked, her accent was just as thick as my father's. They primarily spoke creole. Living in America for twenty-six years they learned to adapt, although their English wasn't perfect they understood and spoke it to the best of their ability.

"The baby is with his mom," I replied.

"We love baby." My mother walked over to the decorative wall unit that was filled with family photos. Grabbing a frame she walked over to me then handed it to me.

Glancing down at the framed photo of Duke, I smiled.

"Baby look like you," she said handing me a few more pictures that she had framed of Duke.

Looking back at my sisters, they acted as if they didn't know how my mother got the photos. I was happy to know that even though my parents wasn't fucking with me that didn't stop them from acknowledging their grandson.

"When you bring baby?" my father asked.

"I'll bring him soon." I sighed.

Now that I've made peace with Stacy, amends with my parents the only thing left for me to do was fix my relationship with Shanika.

*****

"What are you doing here? Lisa is supposed to drop Duke off tomorrow," Shanika said the moment she opened the door.

After our big fight last month, I sent a maintenance crew to her apartment to repair all the damages I made. I even had all the furniture replaced too. Thankfully I was able to pay off the head of security, which in returned he turned the other cheek and didn't call the police or report the damages to the property manager. I didn't want Duke cramped up at Shanika's aunt's house, so I paid whatever I had to pay to make sure her apartment was suitable for my son to live in.

"I need to talk to you."

"You should've called," she deeply exhaled.

"I know, my bad. Can I come in so we can talk?"

"Duke is in his nursery sleeping." Shanika offered as a warning.

"I'm not here on no fuck shit, I swear," I held my hand up.

"Ok." Shanika stepped aside so I could enter the home.

I stood by the door while she closed then locked it, staring at her as she walked to the couch. Something about her was different. Shanika's face looking more fuller, her body a lot thicker. Thicker than how it looked after she gave birth to Duke. I wasn't complaining about that shit though, I was lowkey mad that I wasn't able to hit that every night.

"Ok, so talk." She said pulling me out of my thoughts.

"I never apologized for what went down a few months ago, so I'm sorry," I began, but was distracted by her appearance.

She was glowing. Her hair had grown out some more, it now rested on her shoulder and her had started to spread. When my mother mentioned another baby lizard, I assumed she was talking about Carlene who had revealed that she was expecting but now I was looking at Shanika wondering if she was too.

"I fucked up, really bad and I'm willing to take accountability for my actions and apologize. I want to make amends and fix shit. A nigga real sick without you, ma. I want you and Duke to come home. I want us to be a family, again," I expressed taking a seat on the floor next to her feet.

I was willing to bow down and kiss her feet of that meant should would come home.

"That's all you want?" she asked with a raised brow.

"I want us to be together, too. A committed relationship type shit."

"So, you asking me to be your girl?" she asked with a smile.

"Yea, I mean you need a nigga to spell it out for you?" I chuckled.

"Yup!" she smacked her lips.

Standing to my feet, I made my way to the counter where I found a piece of paper and a pen. I scribbled on it, then handed it to her.

"Will you be my girlfriend? Check yes or yes." Shanika read my note out loud.

"Where is the *no* box?" she asked.

"Saying *no* to a nigga is not an option, I need you and my baby home with me. A nigga suffocating right now and that'll be the only reason I'll be able to breathe."

"I'm sorry too," Shanika said. "I'm sorry for lying to you about scamming and for putting my hands on you, I shouldn't have done that," she admitted.

She didn't apologize for the two niggas she let eat her pussy, but I was going to let her have that since I did say we wasn't in a relationship.

"I accept your apology. I'm willing to let everything go, but I'mma still be on your ass about opening that accountant firm," I truthfully said. I wasn't done distributing weed, but I was slowly transitioning into the dispensary hustle. Either way the money would be flowing in and I didn't need Shanika out here taking chances.

"I already reached out to the realtor you hired, we're looking for a building now," she confirmed with a smile.

"Good," I grabbed her ankles kissing her feet.

"My answer is *yes*. I will be your girlfriend, but I will not put up with you fucking around with other bitches behind my back. So, if you think you won't be able to respect our relationship let me know now, and we can just stick to coparenting."

"I gotchu'," I swirled my tongue between her toes. "I haven't fucked another bitch the entire time we been apart."

"Did you get your dick sucked?"

"Nah. I been jacking my dick to our homemade videos" I truthfully replied. Pussy didn't mean shit when the pussy you really wanted was unavailable. My dick wouldn't even get hard for some of these bitches, that's how big of a hold Shanika had on me.

"We gotta get this right, Haiti. We need you," she said placing my hand on her belly.

"What you tryna say?" I grinned, palming her belly.

"That we're having another baby."

"I knew it!" I beamed, before kissing all over her belly. If I could get her pregnant again right now, I would.

"Why didn't tell me? How far along are you?"

"Eleven weeks. I was going to tell you eventually, I just wanted shit to cool down between us."

"I put that baby in you the day you let me back in that thang," I chuckled. "Whenever we fuck we create a hit, my swimmers don't miss," I gloated, happy that I got my girl and another baby.

Epilogue
Shanika St. Mark

Three years later...

Today was May eighteenth, the day of my birthday and gender reveal. The massive venue was flooded with Haitian flags and other Haitian inspired décor. Loud drums sounded throughout the building while dancer donning striking consumes gracefully danced to the beat. Cora, the event planner didn't miss as she captured the true essence of Haitian Carnival.

Although we were celebrating my birthday, the real purpose of this extravagant event was to gather amongst family and close friends to find out the sex of me and Haiti's rainbow baby, Reign. Three years ago, shortly after me and Haiti reconciled, I miscarried our baby.

For months I was depression. It got so bad that I couldn't look at Duke without crying. Thankfully Haiti was patient with me. It was crazy because that traumatic experience was a pivotal moment in our relationship. The loss of our baby brought us closer together.

Instead of trying for another baby, I got on birth control so we could focus on building. Haiti was still the plug, dealing weed by the pound but he also opened three dispensaries in South Florida and was currently looking into opening one up in California. After helping Lisa open her boutique, I breathed life into *Shanika & Company, CPA*. The first year running my accounting firm was tough, but by the second-year business started booming and I was proud.

"One time for the birthday bitch, two times for the birthday bitch, three times for the birthday bitch, fuck it up of it's your birthday bitch!" Lisa sung, encouraging me to bend over and shake my ass.

Cuffing my ankles, I wobbled my ass while Lisa made sure the long flowy dress she created out of the Haitian flag didn't ride up.

"Man, get up before you make my baby dizzy," Haiti said pulling me up, then wrapping his arms around me.

Turning around, I bent over then started shaking my ass on him. Haiti let me do my thing until the song went off, before handing me a bottle of water so I could hydrate. With this pregnancy, Haiti was very protective. Even though I told him I was out of the danger zone, that didn't stop him from putting me on bed rest. I didn't mind though, I was enjoying working from home and laying under my man all day.

"Are y'all ready to find out what baby Reign is?" Lisa spoke into the microphone.

Haiti and I agreed that no matter what the sex of our baby was, we would name him or her, Reign Pierre. The name was fitting being that he or she was our rainbow baby.

The crowd started cheering, waving their Haitian flags in the air. Glancing back at all our family members I smiled. My aunt—my mother, stood proudly clutching onto Duke's little hand. I was grateful for her. Despite losing my uncle-father last year, she was happy. My aunt had made peace with his death which was why she was able to heal so beautifully. Haiti invested in my aunt's restaurant that she threw all her energy into, so that was doing well.

Haiti's parents were front in center both rocking huge smiles. The moment Haiti introduced me to them, I was welcomed with opens arms. Just like my aunt they were obsessed with Duke.

Next to Haiti's parents were Carlene, her husband and their son. Even Dina stood there impatiently waiting on the gender of the baby. Things between me and Dina started off rocky since she blamed me for being part of the reason Eliza decided to skip town, but we were cool now. We weren't friends or no shit like that but she was welcomed in my home as I was hers.

"Ok drummers lets gooooo!" Lisa said before the six drummers started to beat loudly on their drums.

The dancers circled around the drummers, dancing and clapping to the beat.

"Where is Haiti?" I asked looking around for him, but he was nowhere to be found.

"This nigga about to miss the whole reveal," I irritably mumbled.

"Oh girl, just hush and enjoy the show," Lisa gently nudged me, before hyping the dancers up.

The harder the drummers pounded on their drums; smoke started to fill the air. The smoke filled the air creating a red hue.

"Yessssss! It's a girl! It's a girl!" Lisa was waving a Haitian flag around as she chanted while the crowd cheered.

To match the Haitian Flag Day theme, we decided on blue being for boy and red for girl. I stood there in awe while red smoke filled the air. I was having a little girl.

When the smoked cleared, Haiti was in the middle of the drummers and dancers down on one knee.

"Shut the fuck up!" I shouted, placing my hands over my mouth.

"Shanika," he said handing me a piece of paper that he scribbled on.

Will you be my wife? Yes, or yes?
Chuckling, I nodded my head up and down while tears trickled down my face.

"Yes!" I was finally able to say.

"It looks like we got a fiancé!" Lisa cheered, while Haiti slipped pear diamond engagement ring on my finger.

Standing to his feet, Haiti kissed my lips. Our family members and friends cheered circling around us waving Haitian flags while *Zouk- la sè Sel Médikaman Nou Ni* by the Haitian artist Cassava' loudly played.

"We're having a girl," I said between kisses.

"I know." Haiti smiled.

"You knew?"

"Yup. This gender reveal was a little front so I could propose. I already knew I was having a little girl."

"Did everyone else know?" I asked looking around at everyone wop was getting busy on the dance floor. Nobody was sitting down, everyone was on their feet dancing, even the kids.

"Nah, just me and Lisa."

"So, Lisa knew about the engagement?" I glanced over at her, she was the ringleader dancing on top of the table while hyping everybody up.

"She knew. Now stop with the questions and let's dance." Haiti pulled me on the dance floor as we fell in line dancing alongside our family and friends.

When the DJ switched the song to King Posse, *Retounen,* Haiti chuckled.

"Aye, this the song that was playing when I saw you on that car bent over, shaking yo' ass." he said, bringing me back to the Haitian Flag Day we had what was supposed to be a one-night stand.

"The same day I locked you in, for life." I smirked, waving my hand where the rock laid.

"Had a nigga boo'd up on some Ella Mai type shit. I'm locked in for life, ma" Haiti said sealing the deal with the kiss.

Not only was I *Boo'd up With a Goon from Lil Haiti,* I had his baby, was pregnant with his daughter, and now engaged to that nigga.

The End.

www.ingramcontent.com/pod-product-compliance
Lightning Source LLC
Chambersburg PA
CBHW061428160726

47995CB00003B/799